D1492794

LIFESTYLE CHOICE 10MG

LIFESTYLE CHOICE 10MG

Rosemary Jenkinson

Doire Press

First published in 2020

Doire Press
Aille, Inverin
Co. Galway
www.doirepress.com

Layout: Lisa Frank
Cover design: Triona Walsh

Printed by Clódóirí CL
Casla, Co. na Gaillimhe

Copyright © Rosemary Jenkinson

ISBN 978-1-907682-74-2

All rights reserved. No part of this publication may be reproduced or transmitted in any form or by any means. This book is sold subject to the usual trade conditions.

We gratefully acknowledge the assistance of The Arts Council of Northern Ireland.

LOTTERY FUNDED

CONTENTS

'Woe betide the woman who could sleep with a man and who did not do so!'

— *Zorba the Greek*, Nikos Kazantzakis

MILLENNIAL WOMAN

It's 4.20. I'm composing a list while pretending to work. Suntan lotion, shampoo, condoms… My boss glances over, sensing I'm not doing what I should be doing. He has this sign behind his desk, 'Obstacles are Opportunities'. I'm sure the world does seem pretty opportune when you're on fifty grand a year as he is. Stiofán Ó Muilleoir is his name, but we call him Stevie Miller behind his back.

The office clock clicks round to five. Yesss, and I'm outtahere! Tomorrow, I'm off on holiday to Greece for one whole week. Sun, sea and souvlaki.

'Send us a postcard,' Stiofán calls.

'Sure thing,' I call back, but naturally I won't. The one thing not to do while the head of a handsome Greek rests between my legs is to remember that work even exists.

I feel so light when I go out into the street I swear if a flash mob started dancing I'd even join in. I glance at the shop windows on Royal Avenue as I pass. I could do with a couple of new t-shirts to take. It's always my habit to look at the clothes on the male mannequins as men always get to wear the most comfortable threads — loose clothes are best for the heat. At least my ex, Jake, left me a few t-shirts which I can wear. If I do get a holiday romance, it will hopefully feel like Jake is there witnessing it and feeling heart-broken. I don't have time to shop anyway as I have to meet my housemate, Ryan, in Kelly's Cellars. 'I've something to tell you,' he'd said. I really hope whatever it is doesn't involve him moving out. When Jake left, I was lucky to find such a nice guy to share the rent. Like me, Ryan was seeking refuge from a broken relationship, so it was great to swap sob stories over wine. We've drunk so many bottles together they've had to open a new recycling bank down our road.

He's sitting outside Kelly's Cellars with a glass of wine bigger than a goldfish bowl, looking super-hip in his mirror-glass shades. He really loves a mirror, does Ryan. I'd like to kiss him myself, but the fact he's been seeing quite a few girls on the rebound has put me off. I go through to the bar. My stomach's rumbling, so I order Guinness as it's practically a meal in itself. I might move on to wine after by way of dessert, but I'll wait and see what news Ryan has for me first. There's a diddle-dee-dee session playing in the corner. Diddle-dee-don't. Pint in hand, I go back outside to join Ryan.

He takes his sunglasses off, so I'm guessing it's very serious.

'Do you know Donna?' he asks.

She's the girl he's been with on and off over the past couple of months.

'She's pregnant.'

'Oh my God,' I say.

'Exactly.' His face is a picture of misery. 'Me, a dad. Can you believe it?'

I tell him to breathe. I think of my condoms again and vow to double-check later they're in my suitcase. It doesn't really matter if I forget the suntan lotion as my new Greek man and I will probably spend the whole time in bars.

A tear rolls out of the corner of his eye and I hug him. Donna, of all people. No offence but I'm thinking Donna Kebab every time I see her.

'I don't even love Donna, I love Kate.'

Kate is his ex. She's beautiful and the only reason he left her was because she was pressuring him to start a family. It's incredibly ironic, but I don't dare mention that.

'I might have to move in with Donna,' he says, but I tell him— from a totally selfish viewpoint—he should see how it goes first.

He clearly needs more drink so I suggest moving on to The Cloth Ear. I mean, I like Kelly's Cellars—there's great history: Henry Joy McCracken once hid under a table there, but the trouble is half the clientele end up under the table. It's just not classy enough, end of. I don't like being a snob, but, for God's sake, I'm twenty-nine. My friends are now doing pre-theatre and buying paintings that aren't from IKEA. I really have to start upping my game. That way, even if I still fail in life, at least failure will be something I've achieved rather than something I've just let happen to me.

At The Cloth Ear, we start skulling shots. I notice there are quite a lot of nice men around but I look away when they glance over. Besides, I woke up this morning with psychotic hair—one side was flat and the other stuck out, so I'm not feeling so confident. Or perhaps it's just since Jake that I've lost my confidence with men. That's what he left me with, as well as the t-shirts. Maybe it all stems from my childhood when I had a poster on my wall that said 'Monday's Child is Fair of Face' and I believed it whole-heartedly, until I later found out my Mum had got it wrong and I was born on a Thursday.

The shots are definitely working though. Ryan is eyeing up a dyed-blonde in her mid-forties and asks what I think of her.

'Great. At least you probably wouldn't get her pregnant,' I go and he laughs.

'That's what I like about you,' he says, slapping me on the back.

'You can do the whole sympathy thing and you can still rip the piss out of me like one of the lads.'

I'm not sure being one of the lads is what I'm after but I know what he means. He's far better at flirting than I am. He works as a forklift driver, so I suppose it fits that he can be a pick-up merchant too. Transferable skills they're called. I really should be going home to pack as it's an early flight, but I'm standing there with a drink in each hand — Irish handcuffs, they call them — and it means I haven't a prayer of leaving early. At the bar I meet a businessman, who is as crisp and dapper as the banknotes in his wallet and he buys me another drink. I tell him I'm going to Patmos in the morning. Pat and moss, it even sounds Irish, I say, and after yet another drink I'm half-blocked. It's eleven and I've really got to go or I'm not going anywhere in the morning, except the bathroom.

I look around for Ryan. He's chatting to the hopefully infertile blonde, so I'm quite happy to leave him behind.

It's raining now, a low-level, bone-bedrenching mizzle. I can hear it on the leaves over a kind of alcohol buzz in my head. As I begin to trek up the Lisburn Road, I can smell the kebab houses, fleetingly reminding me of Donna. I'm ravenous. I'm about to duck into one when I hear a voice beside me.

'Hi. Had a good night?'

The voice belongs to a smoking-hot guy in his early twenties with a sexy, floppy fringe. Not that floppy is a good adjective when it comes to a man, but he looks fit in the body. Of course, it's wet and my eyes are a tad blurry, but he seems nice.

'It'd be a great country with a roof,' he quips. We pass a group of girls with their light jackets draped over their heads, joyously singing, 'Hallelujah, it's raining men!' We both laugh. He's an economics student at Queen's, walking up to the Malone Road where he lives with his parents.

'Do you often bring home men you meet on the street?' he asks cheekily.

'Hardly ever. But I could always make an exception. Who knows?'

'Ohhh,' he says, wide-eyed.

I'm loving the delicious tension between us. He looks a bit like a young Michael Fassbender. Michael Assbender. Of course I know it's about to stop when I get to my house. I have yet to pack. Being such a last-minuter is something I have to eradicate from my behaviour if I really want to succeed in life, but I'm in holiday mode and it's like the holiday starts here.

'Shouldn't you be hurrying home to study?' I tease.

'No way,' he says. 'It's only my first year.'

'How old are you?'

'Nineteen.'

Nineteen!

'So how old are you?' he asks.

'Seven.'

'Yeah, right.'

'Officially I am. I was born on February 29th, which means I only have a birthday once every four years. See? Told you I was seven!'

'You're crazy,' he laughs.

At the foot of my street, I stop and I'm about to kiss him goodbye but it turns into a kiss of 'Hello' and 'Come on', and I know it's right as it's time I moved on from Jake. I'm a Millennial Woman, I'm not meant to get strung out on just one person.

'Come on up to my room,' I whisper as we go in the front door.

'Why are you whispering? Is someone here?'

'No one.' I'm feeling like a dope as if I'm whispering for the benefit of Jake who's been gone three months.

Up in my room, my washbag is lying in an oval-mouthed O of reproach. The suitcase is sitting wide open and empty.

'See? No baggage,' I joke but he doesn't get it.

He laughs at my heavy duvets. 'It's like you sleep in a padded envelope.'

The bright light makes me realise I'm still buzzing off my bubble with drink.

We make it to the bed and I start kissing him. Our hair is wet, the back of his head feels like a washed peach. He smells so fresh. We start taking off our clothes and — well, he has a sculptured, perfect body. I'm pretty good too, though I'm a bit slim in the breast region and when my weight's down, I do have the look of a starved whippet. I remember suddenly how Jake didn't appreciate my self-deprecating humour and I think, sod him. I'm in this clinch on the bed and I have these wild, ludicrous visions of taking a selfie right now and putting it on Instagram.

He slides over me. The head of his penis is as round as a pink rosebud, touched by the dew. I'm guiding him in when I suddenly stop, tapping his shoulder like a wrestler.

'Wait.'

'What?' His eyes are already trance-like.

I open my bedside drawer. Quick, quick, quick, I'm telling myself as time is of the essence in these operations or you're back to square one. I finally find the box and take out a condom.

'Here. Put one on.'

He rolls the condom between his fingers before briefly blowing into it, making it rise like a chewing gum bubble. I have no idea what he's doing — he's either checking for punctures or trying to expand it so it fits him better. His hands are febrile with drink and desire but somehow he manages to slip it on. I close my eyes as his flesh merges with mine.

It's almost too quick when he pulls away from me. Maybe it's true that the best things last the least, but, even so, this was fast. The sensation of him quickly ebbs from my body as his head rolls back onto the pillow and his breathing starts to slow. I feel something wet on my inner thigh. Without even looking, I know it's the condom. My hand reaches out and peels it off.

'I better go,' he says, springing up off the bed.

'See?' I say lightly. 'I knew you had to rush home to study.'

As I watch him get dressed, the pregnancy paranoia starts to set in. I get out of bed, pull on my dressing gown and stand at my door to wait for him. It's on my mind to talk about the condom but it doesn't seem the right time for the sharp reality of it. Besides, he's so young I'll have to deal with this on my own. On his way out, he stumbles over my suitcase which is lying there like some kind of giant man trap.

'It's for my trip to Greece,' I explain.

'Nearly went on a trip there myself,' he grins.

We go down the stairs and I open the front door. It's that awkward moment where all these platitudes like 'nice to meet you' are running through my head and we end up staring at each other, clueless. Just as we're standing there, a rotund woman comes up.

'Is Ryan in?'

'No, sorry, he's not.'

Oh, God, it's Donna. I waffle something about him having a couple of drinks with the lads. She doesn't look very happy. She once told Ryan she thought I was sensible. I imagine she's now thinking I'm a terrible influence on Ryan, bringing young lads back at all hours.

'Goodnight,' the guy says, giving me a passionate kiss on the lips.

'Bye now, take care,' I say casually, as if he's a relative who just popped round for a late-night cocoa.

'Do you know where Ryan would be?' Donna asks.

'No,' I say, though I've a good idea who he's with. Even worse, they could even be on their way here right now so I'd better put Donna off sharpish. 'Maybe he's gone clubbing.'

'Just tell him we need to talk,' she says ominously and bounds off into the drizzling dark.

I go back up to my room. I can't believe it. There's Ryan about to be a dad, and I'm potentially pregnant myself to a guy whose name I don't even know! I mean, I've always liked the idea of having kids, and I am genetically pretty good material and lack of breasts aren't important at all, especially if I give birth to a son, but I mustn't have a kid to a total stranger, no, this can't happen at all...

I need a morning-after pill urgently—but I'm off to Greece tomorrow and I'm betting the Boots at the airport has nothing stronger than fifty shades of suntan lotion. Panicking, I rummage in the top drawer for some old contraceptive pill. Microgynon 30. I went on it while I was with Jake, but I stopped as I hated putting chemicals into me. I take one, wondering will it work if I start the course tonight.

I'm not sure. All I know is I'm terrified of being pregnant. I take another.

Then another. And another. And another.

Fuck sake, I've already overdosed. What am I doing?

I quickly look up 'Microgynon overdose' on Google. There's no info anywhere. Obviously I am the only person crazy enough in the world to take five. I've just flooded myself with oestrogen. At least I certainly won't be having a baby now—perhaps not ever! Perhaps I will produce loads of testosterone just to counteract it and I'll turn into a man!

I quickly put a lid on the paranoia. Jesus. On the bright side, I feel sobered up. I'm leaving on holiday in four hours. As I'm still up, I book a taxi. I start packing my case. Jake's t-shirts are about to go in, but...something makes me hesitate. I decide to leave them out.

A flush of nausea waves over me. It must be the Microgynon. I imagine having to call an ambulance. I always thought I'd die comically, maybe from an unwashed grape like your woman said in *A Streetcar Named Desire* or drinking from a beer can that a rat peed on but this is beyond belief.

I calm down and get into bed. Breathe, I tell myself. Tomorrow I will be on a sunny Greek island. It's way too expensive and my credit card's maxed out to the hilt but no matter, it's cheaper than therapy.

I've just turned the lamp off when it hits me — I've forgotten to pack the condoms.

BUTTERFLY'S CANON IN D

T he Promise...

That spring, when I go over to see my parents in England, Mum tells me to look in her notebook. 'It should be next to my cancer book,' she says. *Your Chemotherapy Record* is a booklet in a jaunty bright red, evidently designed to stand out. Beneath it, I find the notebook and leaf to the back page:

> *Want to slip away quietly.*
> *No black.*
> *Informal, a country garden bouquet.*
> *Pachelbel's 'Canon in D'.*
> *23rd psalm.*
> *'Abide with Me' male voice choir.*

Mum's eyesight is failing and she's made me put the lamp on so she can see something of me, but she can still hear me cry.

'Perhaps it's just as well I can't see your wee face,' she says. 'Come on, I'm not ready to go yet.'

'God, I'm no good at all this.'

'You were always a blubberer,' Mum laughs. 'There was a big crying match every time your Dad went away.'

Dad went away to sea for months at a time when I was young and Mum still pokes fun at me for hiding in the wardrobe and crying when he left.

I tell Mum I'm afraid of crying by her bedside during her last days and upsetting her. A whole deathbed scene more sentimental than anything out of Charles Dickens!

'No, you won't,' she says.

I joke that I'm going to read the whole of my collected works, Volumes 1 and 2, by her bedside and she laughs and says, 'Please, no.'

'You don't know how it's going to go,' she says cheerily, looking at me with eyes that hold a promise in them.

The Story...

Things Mum eats:

Victoria sponge

Chips

Custard tart

Madeira cake and custard

Ice cream

Complan

White buttered toast with the crusts cut off

Everything now as pale and milky as baby's milk, as if her tastes are regressing back to her childhood.

I bring Mum in her Complan Original. She can only manage half a glass but it's as refreshing to her as a milkshake. The room's like a furnace, the gas fire is up as hot as it can go but she says it's pleasant. She's naturally 'coldrife', as we call it in Northern Ireland and, even though she feels the cold more now, she wears a light top and cardigan in pale or bright colours, as she always did. Mum still wears black to go out as it's smart but never in the house as she hates dark clothes, just like she hates the dark nights in winter.

'What would you like from the à la carte menu this evening?' Dad asks her ironically, all too aware that he's a basic cook at best. 'Scampi, pizza, fish?' he reels off from his limited repertoire, as Mum passes her tongue over the roof of her mouth, nauseated.

Dad keeps the kitchen door shut as he cooks the dinner. Mum's sense of smell and taste buds are awry, whether from the cancer or the chemo we don't know. Her whole life, she was a great cook, using all sorts of spices and herbs.

'You should have seen the big plate of pasta I ate last night,' she tells me sometimes on the phone and I realise now she's been lying.

I quiz her about the past. It's a feeling of trying to learn quickly from a book before it has to go back to the library.

Years ago, she'd known her own father hadn't much time to live. Shortly before he died, he promised he'd send her a sign after death to tell her all was well. The day before his funeral she was at the kitchen window looking out on my brother and me playing in the garden when she noticed we were surrounded by a host of white butterflies. She went outside to join us and the butterflies covered her too, filling her with a great peace. An hour later, she walked to the bus stop with a book on Irish folklore, planning to return it to the library. A white butterfly followed her all the way. At the bus stop the book happened to fall open on the page where it said that a white butterfly in Ireland signified the soul of the departed.

Dad comes in with scampi and chips for Mum. Only four tiny bits of scampi, a sparse scattering of chips. And, of course, her Osimertinib

40mg Cycle No: 7.

'Sure I'm not worried about my weight,' says Mum, pushing her scampi around her plate. 'I was only seven stone when I was first married. Never did me any harm then.'

Her finger is so thin now she can't wear her wedding ring.

'Eat a bit more,' I urge and she gets pissed off. Sometimes I feel like I'm coping with a recalcitrant toddler. 'Mum, will you give me a sign?'

'If I can, I will,' she says.

'Will it be butterflies?'

'I don't know,' she says. 'But whatever it is, it will surround you…'

What will survive of us is love…

Mum misquotes Larkin. It's actually, 'What will endure is love,' but I like Mum's misremembered version better.

I've bought Mum a birthday card to give to Dad for his 80th. Mum signs it shakily. For Mum, time is measured in family birthdays, celebrations, anniversaries.

'Now I've made James's 80th, I might as well go on to make my wedding anniversary, your 50th, even my 83rd.'

Everything is an unlikely milestone. She's like an athletics champion building up astounding records and achievements. The Usain Bolt of our living room. She's so proud to be alive nearly two and a half years after her terminal lung cancer diagnosis. She claims she is going to Dunach Wood for Dad's 80th, as they always did.

I go upstairs with her. She walks ahead of me in case she falls backwards, as if hauling herself up a rope bridge. She steps slowly, wheezing.

A big oxygen machine has just been installed next to her bed. It makes strange whirring and clunking sounds, a bit like a tumble-dryer. She puts her mask on. It's Dad's and my joke that she looks like she's scuba-diving.

I make sure her pillows are upright. She has to sleep propped up to keep her lungs clear. I am now a pillow-plumper extraordinaire.

Dad is down in the kitchen, having a vodka and talking to himself as he watches the news highlights.

A week later she phones me to say she made it to Dunach Wood and Dad pushed her along in her wheelchair. The oncologist says she isn't to be out in the sun but at this stage I tell her to appreciate the feel of it on her when she can. Her olive skin always adored the sun. She delights in telling me of the time she was young in Italy and all the boys on the beach thought she was Italian too and shouted out, 'Bella, Bella!'

Mum's Next Milestone…

Mum wants my brother, David, to come over from South Africa to see her one last time and he books to come in a few weeks, but Mum is stressing out that she won't make it.

'What am I going to be like at the end of June?' she asks.

'You'll make it,' I assure her.

Her face crumples and she cries. It's so rare she lapses like this.

'I don't want to go. I don't want to leave your Daddy on his own,' she says. 'But there's nothing I can do.'

I wonder out loud how I'm going to cope without her: my confessor, my adviser, my critic, my supporter all rolled into one. She immediately pulls herself together and is calm again.

'This is what I want you to do when I go: stay strong and keep busy.'

There are unexpected pleasures. Mum loves it when the cheery district nurses call in to see her. I enjoy bringing her food. Dad bought her some Tunnock's Teacakes but they're too chocolatey for her, so I crack the surface with a teaspoon like I'm cracking an eggshell and pull the shards of chocolate off, leaving the soft, white marshmallow which she loves.

We still laugh a lot, even when the conversation turns dark. Dad says that when he feels it's his time to go, he's going to go out into the garden one night with a bottle of vodka and let the cold take him.

'No, you're not,' says Mum, outraged at what the neighbours might think. 'You'll leave the bottle in the kitchen where no one can see it!'

I like to watch over her. Her eyes tiny now under her more feral eyebrows. Sometimes her face is in deep concentration as she attempts to sleep and you can never tell if she is resting or asleep. Often she senses my shadow at the door and opens her eyes. She can't see if it's me or Dad, so I call out to her. To be honest, I'd like to sit at the end of her bed like a benign angel, listening to her deep chesty breathing, just marvelling at the life in her, but I know she would get pissed off and tell me to go.

Mum is quite content except for when she has to go for a scan.

'I have to see the oculist next week,' she says, troubled.

'The oncologist you mean,' and we laugh.

Her words are starting to slip a little, her breathing won't let her deliver the syllables. She's coughing a lot.

The oncologist offers her a temporary break from the chemo to try and get her eating on track, which she gratefully accepts. When she sees the respirologist, he agrees to give her portable oxygen cylinders. Then he shakes her hand and says goodbye with no further appointment. Mum takes this as a sign.

Mum's Advice...

'Write free like a bird, don't think of anyone when you write. Don't be too aloof, too bolshy or too cold.'

The next week when I'm at someone else's play, I'm the only

person who won't stand up for a standing ovation and I think to myself, Jesus, Mum's right. I am too bolshy.

I cry a bit when I see her again.

'Sorry,' I say.

'Oh, it's fine. I'm kind of used to you now. So, how do I look?'

She looks thinner and more ashen than before, but she has showered and blow-dried her hair especially for me coming, a task that I know has taken her and Dad long, arduous hours, and rouged her hollow cheeks.

'You look well. Brighter than before.'

'Yes, I'm keeping it up,' she says delightedly.

Outside, I keep hearing doves loudly cooing.

'It's a pair of turtle doves,' says Mum happily. 'There were loads living here a few years ago, but then they all went away. This year, just one couple came back. They're nesting in our rhododendron bush.'

It's time for her chemo and her medicine that cuts the phlegm. Dad pours the liquid into the cap and hands it to her.

'Cheers! Bottoms up,' he goes, grinning, and she puckers her face up with the taste.

Later, I walk in on them as Dad is hovering over her. Mum is complaining.

'What are you two doing?'

'We're having sex,' Dad replies tartly and I feel like an idiot for asking.

What Dad is really doing is injecting Mum's thigh to prevent blood clots. Her skin is badly bruised from daily injections.

'Ah, he's so good, aren't you?' Mum says. 'I don't know how he bears me. He'll soon have had enough.'

'Just watch out when one day he suggests bringing you out in the wheelchair on the cliffs.'

'Oh, I know,' laughs Mum. 'Or my medication suddenly doubles in dosage!'

I wake up at three that night. The sky is lightening. The blackbirds and song thrushes are whistling. The turtle doves are cooing again joyously, thrilled that the night is so short. Or maybe like me they just can't sleep. I can hear the low murmur of Radio 4, which keeps Mum company all through the night.

He shall cover you with his feathers...

When my brother David comes, I fly over too. David tells me he was shocked when he saw her and he's certain it's the last time he'll see her this side of eternity. Mum sits in the living room, feeling the draught. My brother lives in South Africa, the big, hot wide open, so he can never remember to shut the door.

Mum's a lot calmer and happier with him there. He's told her she'll be painting up in heaven. And she'll be making nice food. I didn't think they ate up in heaven, but perhaps they do. He reads to her from the Bible every morning. Her favourite is Psalm 91:

'He shall cover you with his feathers, and under his wings, you shall find refuge: his truth shall be your shield and buckler.'

When I was recovering from my back operation a few years ago, she used to read it to me too.

Mum's head is lying in a box. Not her actual head; a sculpture that David brought down when he was clearing the roof space. It's sitting there in her bedroom like Marie Antoinette's guillotined head. Her friend made it at art school when she was nineteen. She looks young and her hair is impeccable. 'You can have it,' she says. Great, I think. I'll be the only person to have their mother's head in a box. I can't imagine David will be fighting me for this particular family heirloom.

'My friend and I were the only ones recommended to go to art college in London, but I couldn't go as Daddy had no money,' she says and it's the closest moment to regret I've seen before she spins it away. 'But Daddy got ill a few years later, so it was just as well I stayed.'

I pull out the sketch pads and paintings from under the bed and flick through her pastels and watercolours and oils, some half-finished, describing to her what I see.

She has a small green stone which she keeps at her bedside. The minister picked it up from the shingle beach of Iona. She presses the stone devoutly to each of her eyes and to her chest, holding it there, mirroring the hardness clinging to her inner right lung.

I know that Mum thinks we will all be together in heaven but what worries me is that we'll all be scattered across different parts of it — just as Mum and Dad are in England, I'm in Northern Ireland and David's in South Africa.

Whatever it is, it will surround you…

It's two weeks after my brother left. Dad is up and down those stairs so much, it's like he's doing step aerobics.

It's cold in Mum's room. She doesn't like to sleep in a warm room as she can't get a breath. The turtle dove is high on our roof proclaiming his love. I too want a life where my only regret is dying. I go out for a walk, enjoying the high summer. The butterflies are out in full force: the red admirals and a few white ones. I pluck a red flower that's wildly straying through a gap in someone's fence and bring it home to show Mum a glimpse of summer. It has no scent, so I know it won't make her cough.

'Where did you get it?' she asks sharply, as if I'd stolen it.

She can hardly see it and she's disinterested anyway. There's no season in her room, though I've always known she would die in summer as it's the time of year she most loves.

She's so tiny in her bed. The more Mum shrinks the more I want to hold her. She was born prematurely and was laid in a drawer lined with cotton wool to help her survive. Just like she's now almost encased in the thick, white pillows.

Her cough's getting worse and the antibiotics are failing to kick in. When she coughs now, she coughs up more and more sticky fluid. I get her a bowl to spit into. Dad orders her a commode as it's hard for her to get to the bathroom now. One night she fell and hurt her hip.

I carry up the photos of the ancestors. Old black and white photos of her parents as children. She can hardly see them but she knows the photos by memory and tells me who's who. Just a last inventory of the past.

I stay a couple of days, and she seems to be sleeping a lot of the time, but just half an hour before I'm due to leave I hear her cry out to Dad. She couldn't make it out of bed for the bathroom and she's soiled herself. I peel off her nightie, help Dad to change the sheets. She's shy because she's such a private person.

'I don't want your last memory to be of this,' she says, embarrassed, and I say, 'What? This is nothing!' I remind her of the time she had bladder problems at David's wedding and she peed on the back seat of the car when she was sitting right next to me.

'Aw, don't be remembering that,' she laughs.

'Mum, you're not God, you're a human body,' I tell her, 'And it's all fine.'

She holds on to me and her hand still feels so strong. She asks for a soft table mat, just to lay under her to protect the sheet in case of another accident. I quickly take out a beautiful one made by David's South African wife.

'You can't use that,' Mum objects. 'It's too good.'

'Mum, does it really matter any more?'

'I don't suppose it does.'

'I have to go now, but any time you need me, just call and I'll be over straight away.'

'Alright now.'

We have a last hug and I tell her with passion how much I love her. I can hear something breathing in her chest; every time she's talking it's like a person is trapped deep within her. It's the same sound I heard when she was first diagnosed with lung cancer and it makes my blood run cold.

'Remember—it's not goodbye, it's farewell!' Mum calls out chirpily as I go.

I look back at her. The sketch pads seem to be almost bulging out beneath the base of her bed, and the last image I am left with is of her lying, raised up, on her art.

MEN

In my life I'd had about five boyfriends and one abortion. I was twenty-six years old and my family said I hadn't met the right person. I didn't think there was a right or wrong person for me, they were all just different. A person was right one day, and the next he was wrong.

I'd had a near collision with marriage once, about five years ago. I'd had this ridiculous naïve pride that no man would ever want to finish a relationship with me, but my fiancé did on the grounds of my infidelity, which he found out through reading my diary. Afterwards, half of me hoped he'd get over me and find the woman he deserved, and the other half hoped he'd be embittered for ever. I never heard of him again. For a long time after, every time I saw a reminder of him — an old letter, a photograph, a book he'd bought me, it affected me...

Joe had tight curly, black hair, the whitest teeth and nice green eyes. They were sad-looking eyes because he had top-heavy eyelids, but it wasn't his nature. He liked all the lads' things, like drinking beer and playing pool, but his most favourite was watching Newcastle play football on the box and yelling abuse at the screen. For all his braying over football, I liked his laidback character and he knew how to treat women well, which was why I agreed to move with him from Newcastle to Gillingham.

Perhaps it was the drink that united us. We both signed on the dole in Gillingham, and his Mum, who was living locally, found him a job working cash-in-hand as a barman. When it was a sunny afternoon and all the customers were outside, he'd ring me to come over and pour me free beers. He was thoughtful like that. We got on fine.

In three months' time he was due to start work as a trainee pub manager with a big brewery. I think his mother, Nikaya, had some half-cocked idea that Joe and I were going to get married in the near future. I didn't like Nikaya much. She was always touching the breasts of a big rugby player who came into the pub. Joe's stepfather, Ivan, was usually drunk and obnoxious and his backside teetered on the edge of the barstool. The previous year he'd successfully won compensation from another pub when he'd fallen off his barstool and broken his leg.

The times Joe worked in the bar, I was writing in our run-down, rented bungalow. My words were gradually materializing into a love story about scum/salt of the earth — in my experience there was no intrinsic difference between the two and it depended on perspective, like most things. I would start with a beer every morning, then quickly drink down a coffee. The way I looked at it, the beer loosened my hangover from the night before, relaxed me, and the coffee would keep me awake. It seemed to work. I was fairly romping through the pages. Fifteen, twenty pages a day. Joe had bought me a second-hand computer. He was a great guy really.

I had a provisional title — 'Life is Everywhere' by Tara Shaw. It felt reassuring to write it down. It gave a touch of tangibility to the airiness of it all. Writing to me felt unreal. It terrified me. I half-expected the letters to crawl off the page one night and join the woodlice which kept creeping in under the back door.

One afternoon we were sitting on the sofa in the front room while Joe read my work.

'Who is this guy you're writing about?'

'No one. Just a composite.'

'Is it an ex?'

'No. It's a literary combination of — of Mr Darcy and Alfie.'

Oh, right. So, you're telling me this Mr Arsey doesn't exist?'

'Yes, so don't feel inferior to him.'

'Me, I wouldn't feel inferior to a paper cut-out, Tara. But you didn't make these sex scenes up, did you?'

'Don't you believe I have an imagination? Don't you credit me with anything?'

If he was going to go on in this vein, there was going to be a scene.

'Imagination,' he scoffed.

'What's eating you, anyway? You can't expect to have been the first.'

'I won't play second fiddle to anyone.'

He looked sulky.

'Come on, Joe. Who could compete with literature?' He looked away and I was pissed off too. 'Yeah, well, great. I'm hungry. Will you make me a bacon sandwich?'

He got up and walked out of the room but not in the direction of the kitchen. After a few minutes I followed him into the bedroom. He was lying on the bed and I flopped down beside him, putting my arm around him.

'Want to fuck?' I asked.

He groaned but there was a promising glimmer of a grin.

I shook him roughly. 'Well. Anything wrong still?'

He gave me that wide-toothed sexy smile. 'I just thought I was what you liked.'

'Baby, you are. I love you.'

We kissed. I made a mental note to make all future sex scenes sound more like those Joe and I enjoyed.

The reading of the sex scenes seemed to prey on Joe's mind. They made him dig deep into his subconscious, perhaps even inspired him. The next night he told me his deepest sexual fantasy. I was surprised but I said we could try sometime. It made a change from the simple fetish of wanting his back scratched during sex. Like a lot of people, Joe had a thing to get off on. People have something done to them once in sex and they make a habit of it. In my opinion it was a bit dull but at least it made you easily satisfied.

This hidden desire, however, I understood. I always thought there was a touch of the woman in Joe. He was quite fleshy, curvaceous even which maybe sounds unfitting in a man but was quite a turn on, something different. His mother had been voluptuous (now pendulous), his sister was gorgeously voluptuous, adored by all men, and he was a masculinized version of the same. I liked the fact that he was even shapelier than me, and he had really fine legs. I wasn't so narrow-minded to have a 'type' of man I liked.

And I didn't think it was odd to want your girlfriend to fuck you.

The bar was completely packed as it always was on a Saturday afternoon. The only seat left was next to Joe's stepfather, Ivan. There was often a seat left next to Ivan. He was drunk as usual. It was riveting to watch him. Looking into his eyes, though, tended to make you feel seasick, so it was better to focus just above them.

'Less than two months,' he said, 'till Joe starts his new job at the pub.'

'Is that all?' I hadn't thought about it.

'Do you really think you can be a landlady? Do you think that you'll be able to cope with it for the rest of your life?'

The rest of my life? I'd never thought about the whole landlord scenario in relation to me.

'Sure, I can manage anything,' I said to Ivan breezily. It was none of his business. It was bad enough my own family going on about what I was going to do with my life.

'It's a hard life, you know. How do you think you'd manage with the customers?'

He was just rubbing it in now. He knew I didn't like him. 'I'd be nice to the nice people and horrible to the fuckers.'

'More complicated than that, Tara. You have to charm them all.'

It was a lot more complicated than that, Ivan, because I wasn't bloody doing it. I was born on this side of the bar. I was bad enough for a drink without having twenty-four hours access to a million gallons worth downstairs.

An hour later, I caught him by the arm as he nearly toppled off the stool.

'You know what I would do with you, Ivan, if you came to my pub? To make you stay upright, I'd tie your wrists together and lash you to the pump.'

'I never told you, Tara, but I'm glad you're with Joe,' he said soppily.

Joe's Mum interrupted us by appearing from nowhere, in the way that the sober always seem to teleport themselves into your company.

'Hello, my sweet,' cried Ivan, trying to embrace her.

She pushed his hands away roughly. 'Don't my-sweet me, you old sot. You said you'd pick me up at four. That was two hours ago.' She lifted up two supermarket bags from the floor. 'I can't put that in the freezer now. Eh? It's all melted. What are we supposed to do with all that fish? Suck it up through a straw?'

'She likes sucking, don't you, Nikaya?'

Nikaya whacked him across the back of the head. This time I let him fall to the floor.

The whole bar was gaping. Joe behind the bar looked embarrassed.

'I wish you were coming too tonight.'

Joe was doing his tie up. He had the shakes, so I stood behind him and tied it. It looked good, the dazzling white shirt against his lightly tanned skin. He filled the shoulders of the jacket and the material was tight between his shoulder blades.

'You should wear a suit more often, Joe.'

Ivan had decided he'd make a big thing of his son's thirtieth birthday and have a party in London with all his sons. They were going to stay overnight.

'I asked Ivan if you could come but he said he didn't want any women there.'

'Why? What's he got in store for you? Brothels?'

'No way. One of his sons is gay.'

'A gay brothel then. Maybe you'll be in Soho.'

'You do trust me, don't you?'

'Sure. I know it must be a male family bonding thing. In the old days you would have gone hunting or fishing, now you go trawling round the clubs.'

'Trawling. There'll be no trawling.'

'I know. I'm joking.'

He checked his watch.

'What will you do tonight, Tara?'

'Go to the pub.'

'Yes. *The* pub. Not just any old pub.'

'Of course, I meant *the pub where you work.*'

'Yes, you'll be fine there. You know lots of people.'

'I know.'

Finally he left and I cracked open a beer and made a sandwich. I didn't know what the big deal was about him going to London. He could be a bit clinging.

I wasn't writing any more. It had taken me just four weeks to write the novel. I'd fired it off to a dozen publishing houses and agents. I was semi-happy with it—it had a recognizable start, middle and end, but I wondered if I hadn't verged on the fantastical side of things. I wondered if really I was qualified enough to write a love story. Someone who used the word *clinging* probably wasn't on a wavelength with monogamous love.

There was a ring at the door at about seven.

It was Phil who drank at the pub.

'Hi, Phil.'

He planted a broad hand on the wall, lazily leaning his weight on it.

'Hi, Tara. Heard you were alone tonight.'

'That's right.'

News travelled fast. He smelt like he was doused in aftershave. It was a potent mix with the scuffed, shiny slip-on shoes and the shirt unbuttoned to show a wide piece of chest. I've always had a thing for vampish men.

In the pause, he spoke again.

'I've come to take you to the pub.'

'I'll be over in a few minutes. You go on.'

I closed the door over, breathing out long and hard. It didn't take the vultures long to circle and I quietly applauded my own strength of will. I could see the tousled bed through the bedroom door.

I was in the pub before half-seven. Phil was drinking hard.

As the sun began to lower, I went into the garden. Nikaya was sitting there at a crowded table. She looked pretty relaxed and happy with the world. The rugby-playing hulk was sitting beside her. He'd taken his shirt off revealing a chest as muscled and hairless as a Roman breastplate, his skin turning bronze in the setting sun. Nikaya reached over and squeezed one of his breasts and everyone laughed with her. I wondered what was going on in London.

I joined the guys who played in the pub pool league with Joe.

One was showing us the scars from putting his fist through a glass door after his wife had said she was leaving him.

He was crazy. With scars from love, he'd never stand a fresh chance. Men and their scars. They were all crazy.

Someone nudged me.

'Hello, Phil.'

'Me and Dave, we've been watching you all night, Tara, and have just voted you Rear of the Year.'

'That's very kind of you. Excuse me a minute.' The Rear of the Year escaped to the rear of the pub where I got chatting to some people.

'Have you ever had outdoors sex?' one girl asked me.

'Oh, loads,' I said.

'Instead of sex on the beach, it's sex under a beech,' said a guy called Max.

'I've made love in many beds, even a flowerbed,' I rejoindered.

'Under a willow,' the girl said dreamily. 'A willow's so erotic.'

'A pussy willow,' giggled Max and his wife dug him in the ribs.

Closing time rolled around and we were blitzed.

'Fancy coming back to ours?' Mad Max asked about six of us. 'Got some cans and some blow left.'

'I'm not feeling so good, Max,' his wife, Daisy, said.

'Well, I feel like a drink,' he said. 'Who's up for it?'

I was and so was another guy called Michael.

Max said it wasn't far to walk. After about a mile, Michael decided to pull out and go home. Max had his arm round Daisy and was practically dragging her up the road.

'Maybe I'll go back too,' I said.

'It's round the corner. Come on,' Max said briskly.

I had only met Mad Max twice before. He was about thirty and highly eccentric. He held down some high-powered computing job in London but he had the whackiest appearance. His hair was like some windswept, eighteenth-century composer's and he wore hippy clothes like tie-dyed shirts and Jesus sandals. His jeans were drainpipes and tight round the crotch, cradling the cutest little ass. But because he was so off-the-wall, so unnaturally energized like he was constantly on speed, you didn't think of him sexually, and his wife was plain and dumpy. He was on a hundred grand a year or more and he drove an orange camper with a Union Jack in the window stitched with the words, 'Be Happy'. That was Max.

It was about another mile to his house. I was stumbling everywhere and becoming oblivious to Max's pioneering spirit. Daisy hadn't said a word the whole way. Suddenly her head went forward and she puked on her shoes.

'It's all right. Not far now,' said Max.

We finally got there. I was happily aware of entering a paradise of billowing, tie-dyed sheets and high-ceilinged yellowness. Max was lighting some joss-sticks while I rested on the settee.

'Here's your beer,' he said. 'Come down with me.'

I sat on a cushion on the floor beside him. He rolled a joint in double-quick time. I'm sure I could have taken over the world if I'd had his energy.

'Have you ever played—?' He uttered some Asian word.

'No. It's not some contact sport, is it? Or I warn you, I'll do a Daisy.'

He jumped up, went over to a glass-fronted cabinet full of empty shelves and pulled down a box sitting on top of it. Everything in the house was close to hand. I marvelled at the organized chaos, the inside-out cosmogony of Mad Max.

Pieces of wood tumbled out onto the floor. Max put a low table between us.

'This is how it works. I'll build it up, then we take turns to take pieces out without knocking the whole lot down. Okay?'

'Seems a bit complicated, Max.'

He'd left a joint in the ashtray, leaving the smoke to fly into the air, so I rescued it and took a few sharp tugs to resuscitate it back to full life.

'I've got a terrible headache,' Daisy groaned. I looked round and she was standing at the living room door like a ghost in a nightdress with a glass of water in her hand and a foiled pack of headache tablets. She looked dreadful. 'Goodnight.'

'Goodnight,' I said.

Max waved without looking up. He was swiftly building a miniature tower. Once he'd finished I managed to extract a piece of wood from the middle.

'Don't you see how my hands are shaking?'

'You want another beer?'

'I'm still on this one.'

'Why? What's the matter with you?' He took off his t-shirt to reveal his bare chest.

'Are you hot?'

'Very. I'll tell you how we'll make this game more interesting. Every time one of us takes a piece out, that person takes an item of clothing off.'

'Not me.'

He passed me another beer and smiled. 'More beer, no fear.' He rubbed his hands together, concentrated and slid a piece of wood out from the base of the tower. Then he undid the buttons of his tight jeans and rolled them down his legs. His underwear slipped off with his jeans. He was naked. Shorn of his odd-fashioned clothes, he was a different man. His body was lean and perfectly toned. His cock was semi-erect and already big. His unkempt hair looked attractively wild.

'Max, in coming here, my doors of perception have been truly cleansed.'

'Why don't you take your clothes off?'

'What if Daisy comes down?' I had this horrible image of her pale ghostly form coming down the dark stairs like an avenging spirit.

'She won't. She's gone to bed. Come on. There doesn't have to be anything heavy between us.'

I took my clothes off fast. I couldn't help laughing at the situation and Max was laughing too. I looked into his face. He had full cheeks, dark eyes and lips fatter on one side making him look like a devilish cherub.

'We'll start with this,' he said, taking hold of my foot. He pressed the soles of my feet with his thumbs. 'This is Asian medicine.'

'Ah, this is the Asian game you meant us to play.'

He grinned. 'Come in, come in to my massage parlour, said the spider to the fly.'

He cupped his hands around my foot gently. He softly kissed the base of my toes and I quivered at his breath and the coolness of his tongue. He then kissed my ankle, working his way up my leg. He pushed back the folds of skin round the clitoris, like he was delicately pushing back the closed petals of a flower and began to lick. I felt the numbness and intensity, the pins and needles and the pressure growing and my foot kicked over the wooden tower. God, he was good. I pulled his head into me, till I could feel the power of his jaw working on me and the desperate sounds of breathing and finally I came with a flood of shaking.

I pushed him away and started sucking on his cock which was already hard. I nibbled the tip, then sucked up and down the sides. His hips rocked gently up and down. He was propped up on his elbows watching as his cock went in and out of my mouth. He kept giving moans of excitement. I felt the tremors in his legs and pulled with my hand faster and harder, hearing the roar of my own breath in my ears as my tongue swirled and flicked. I heard him gasp explosively. I looked up at his anguished face and a flood of warmth rushed into the roof of my mouth. I let go and released his come from my mouth into the palm of my hand. I walked into the kitchen and washed it down the sink.

He held his arms open to me when I came back.

'You don't swallow?'

'No. I wouldn't swallow a raw egg white either. It's one of my little puritanities.'

'Purit—?'

'Puritanities as distinct from profanities.'

'I'd like to know more of your profanities,' he said, rubbing my clit gently with the backs of his fingers. As he touched me, he let out little deep-throated murmurs as if he could feel the effect of his own fingers on my body. We kissed and I moved his cock to the mouth of my vagina.

'No,' he said.

Either he was scared of me getting pregnant or the oral sex had been one of those mental safety nets, a self-imposed boundary where copulation was infidelity. The irony was that if he thought he was giving a uniquely special place to his wife by fucking only her, she mightn't make the same distinction if she came down and saw us licking away at each other like dogs on bones. There were no half freedoms in this world.

We lay locked together on the floor for a long time, just touching, fingers on assholes, tongues together. I kept falling asleep while we touched and dreaming of his face beside me and when I awoke seconds later, his face was even closer and I couldn't tell if I was in this world or still in the other. It was beautiful to feel his breath on my face.

'I'll have to go up to Daisy now.' Max leapt up. After that little bit of calm, his energy was back.

'I know.'

I got dressed. I hadn't got my land legs back at all and I had trouble finding a sock. Max looked everywhere for it.

'There it is,' he said, slapping me on the butt. It had got caught between my buttocks and my jeans when I'd put them on.

Max didn't offer to call a taxi, so I presumed it was safe and took the long walk home. It was after three-thirty and there was a little light in the sky. It was an incredibly warm night.

A week later I'd got most of the manuscripts back with no comment other than the publishers' or agents' lists were full. It seemed to me odd that literature had to have a set quota like petrol or grain. One publisher scribbled me a note, 'Dear Tara Shaw, I enjoyed the first chapter! You obviously have a strong imaginative vision. However, I'm afraid we're not going for this one.' As I'd suspected, my realism was a little too fantastical. That was my own brand of reality and I couldn't help it. The bungalow was too damp even though it was summer. There were loads of black stains on the walls. The damp had maybe got into my brain.

Whatever the case, I was going to have a rethink.

Joe hadn't said much at the time about me going to Max's house. A week later he brought it up again.

'Oh, I meant to tell you, I was talking to Michael yesterday and he said he didn't go with you to Max's.' His tone was carelessly casual.

'That's right. I remember now. He said he was coming to Max's, then he baled. I was totally rat-arsed. As I said, there were a couple of other people who came.'

'Like who?'

'Can't remember.' He stared at me, forcing me to tax my imagination into making up more useless fucking fiction. 'Some dark-haired guy and his blond girlfriend.'

'Oh. Do they drink often in the pub?'

'I don't think so.'

'Funny. Michael said no one else went.'

'That's because they had to pop home first before going to Max's.' I tried to match casual tone for casual tone. 'They came later. How would Michael know anyway? He was more out of his skull than I was.'

It looked bad and I knew it. Joe was many things — too watchful, too jealous and his greatest crime was that he loved me. There was something I owed to us both. That I wouldn't let the rats inside us gnaw this relationship to death.

That week we went to London.

We had a good drink, then took our pick of the sex shops in Soho. We went into some kind of pink den and had a look at the dildos hanging up on the wall. They were sixty quid. As we had a drink habit to maintain, it seemed a tad extravagant. If we could have test driven them first, we might have considered it.

'There's one for forty,' Joe said, pointing to a puny piece of plastic.

'I have my pride,' I told him. 'Size matters.'

We looked along and got to these hollowed-out plastic cocks which had nobbled surfaces. The price tag said fifteen pounds.

'Is that for the man to wear?' I asked Joe.

'How would I know?'

'Well, what we could do is fill it with something hard and then it's a dildo.'

Joe looked dubious.

'It's only fifteen pounds,' I said. 'We'll take it.'

The man at the cash desk wrapped it up.

'It's the time of the year for it, isn't it?' he said. He was very camp. His lips visibly minced as he spoke. We said yes though we hadn't a clue what he was talking about.

'Our summer sale starts next week, you know. You two should come. We have all sorts of bargains.'

He looked at Joe up and down. I wondered if what we'd bought was a plaything worn by gay men. And perhaps by gay men with small penises who couldn't satisfy their lovers normally. It wasn't a nice sensation being innocents in the big city.

We took the train home that afternoon. We had a couple of hours before Joe was due to start work at the pub. While Joe showered, I sat in the front room and began to fill the plastic cock with crumpled up newspaper. No matter how much newspaper I stuffed in, it was still kind of bendy.

Joe kissed the back of my neck.

'Come on,' he said.

We stripped and I stepped into the elastic straps. He stretched out on the sofa and I jumped on. We kissed and my hand reached out for his cock and he started fingering my clit. I found I was really excited. I couldn't wait—I was about to get his cherry. I wanted to see his face when I was really giving it to him, the lines in his forehead, his perfect teeth bared. I dropped down and took some hard tokes on his cock. He let out a series of moans. Then I pushed his hips up and started licking his asshole. When it was moist I stuck my fingertips in. It was very tight. After a while he relaxed and moaned again.

I tried to thrust the cock up against his arse. I had absolutely no control over it. The straps were evidently built for a man and they were falling off me, slipping down my thighs. There weren't any devices for tightening it either. I didn't want to spoil the moment so I just grabbed the thing and pushed it in between his buttocks.

He cried out. 'Gently!'

I made some gentle pushes. The giant bendy head was nowhere near going in, so I gradually became more forceful.

'Stop!'

'What?'

'Look,' said Joe, clapping his hands over my ass. 'Fucking hell!'

The doorbell suddenly rang and I followed his scared eyes to the window.

There was a guy standing looking in at us. He must have been in his early twenties, one of those chugger types with a red lanyard and a clipboard, trying to save some species of human or animal. Another guy who'd just rung the bell came and joined him. It wasn't that they were being unlawfully nosy. It was just the bad architecture of the bungalow to have the front door half a metre from the window. That and the fact the net curtain was ripped. Usually we heard the gate if anyone was coming but we'd forgotten to close it.

'Bollocks. Go out and give them some money, Joe.'

One of the guys was pulling the other away from the window by his lanyard.

'You're joking! They should be paying us for a performance like this.'

They were gone, so I moistened the head of the cock and nudged it in again.

'Tara.'

'Yes?'

'I don't like it. It's too painful.'

'Okay.' I climbed off.

It reminded me of a perfectly straight guy I once knew who said he'd always wanted to experience sleeping with a man. One night we happened to meet a gay guy on the train home who also happened to be getting off at the same stop as us. I invited him back to ours for a coffee and, a second later, I was being dragged by the arm up the street.

'Not him,' said the guy. 'I don't like him. He's too camp.'

Funny thing about some men. They have vast imaginations yet they don't have the balls to do anything. Maybe there was just too much pressure in the world to be sexually adventurous. I kind of liked straight sex myself. You would think people would concentrate on getting the most out of it first, before launching off into flights of fancy.

'Are you pissed off with me, Tara?' Joe asked.

'No. Who cares?' I squeezed his knee. 'We have plenty of drink money. And we have each other.'

Joe and I came back from the pub and took the cans out of the fridge. Joe rustled up some noodles and bunged in the soy sauce. There was gymnastics on the TV.

'They've got some strength,' said Joe.

They were so delicately pale-faced but muscled, like they'd been grown in a laboratory of perfection. A Russian gymnast in white was on the rings doing the crucifix position. The muscles under his ribcage rippled and his arms shook. I could have taken him on the cross then and there.

'It's your birthday next week,' said Joe.

'I know.'

'Twenty-seven,' he grimaced. He was a twenty-five-year-old puppy.

'It's all right. I'm not yet at my sexual peak. You on the other hand have passed yours.'

'Sex is an ageless state of mind. Anyway, what do you want for your birthday?'

'A pair of jogging bottoms.'

'I can't get you that! What would you really like?'

'Why not jogging bottoms?'

'Well, it's not romantic. I can't tell everyone I bought you that.'

'Do you need audience approval? Look, it's what I need. The beauty is that we can both wear them.'

'No! Something else.'

I shrugged. 'Lacey bra and pants then,' I grinned. 'The beauty is that we can both wear them.'

'That's enough of that rubbish. I was thinking more of jewellery.'

Joe's mobile rang and he answered. 'Mam.' He went very quiet. 'Are you sure?' he asked. 'Stay there. I'm coming over now.' He leapt to his feet.

'What?'

'Come on. It's Mam. She's killed Ivan.'

He ran out the front door and I was left to lock up. I ran after him. I could see him in the distance, sprinting away from me.

The door to the house was open. I could hear Nikaya talking hysterically.

I walked in. Joe was kneeling on the floor beside Ivan. 'It's all right, Mam. Don't call the police. He's alive. He's just out cold.'

'Thank God!' Nikaya sighed. 'I was sure I'd brained him. Are you positive we don't need an ambulance?'

'Look.' Joe pulled back his eyelids. 'His eyes are moving.'

'Christ!' said Nikaya. 'It's like something out of *The Exorcist*.'

'He's got a hell of a bump on his head,' said Joe. There was a heavy glass ashtray on the floor by his feet. 'What made you do it?'

'I was furious. Ivan accused me of having an affair with Alex. I just lost it.'

Alex was the rugby player.

'Mam,' said Joe.

Joe was quiet as we walked home. He suddenly burst into laughter. 'What a carry on! Wait till I tell my Dad that she thought she'd killed Ivan.'

'Did she ever injure your Dad?'

'Not that I recall. Just mentally.'

He pulled me into the bedroom when we got home and drove in his cock without foreplay.

'Go easy, honey,' I said because I was dry and it hurt. 'There's an entry speed.'

'I haven't got a driving licence,' he said and he rived it in again.

He spun me over till I was on top, put his arms around me, pulling me down onto his chest, and thrust at top speed. All my juices flooded out and he slapped me again and again against his belly. Even though he was fleshy he had a hard bone and my clitoris hit against it and scratched on the pubic hairs, making it alive. There was a beautiful sound, like the lapping of the sea against a harbour wall. I started juddering faster and faster on top of him and finally he came.

'Give me a second,' I said. I knew I wouldn't be able to sleep, so I turned face-down to finish it off. Joe put his finger in and out my cunt and in a minute I had come.

'Amazing,' he said.

It was true I was untypical. First, although I was right-handed, I masturbated with my left hand, all the sensitivity being on the right side of my clitoris. Also, I only masturbated face-down, a legacy of sharing a room as a child and biting the pillow to muffle my excited breathing. Joe had said in soft porn women always masturbate face-up, so he'd assumed that's how all women did it, as if they were doing it for the camera.

It was my birthday and we were sitting in the Indian. I had on my new ring, Joe's present, and I was wearing the one dress I owned. The dress was on only its third outing. The type of people I associated with didn't get married or have formal parties. It wasn't dresses I disliked, it was the shoes you were expected to wear with them. You had to drink more to forget about them.

'We'll be moving into the rooms above the pub in about five weeks. I hope it's good,' Joe was saying.

I put down my fork.

'What's wrong?'

'Joe, listen. I didn't want to tell you before, but I'm not coming.'

'What?'

'I'm sorry. I hate to hurt you but I've decided. I'm going abroad.'

'Where?'

'Don't know yet, but I'm going soon.'

'One second.' He looked into my eyes. 'Does this mean we can never see each other again?'

'Of course, we'll see each other again. You'll come and visit me. And I'll always wear this,' I added, looking at the ring. 'I'll miss you.'

'I'll miss you too.'

Our six months together were finished within a few words. He took it well. Stoically. He'd known all along I couldn't run a pub with him. Though he didn't say it, he knew deep-down that I didn't care for family, that I couldn't stop looking at men and I got bored in one environment. Like a flower, I required constant replanting and different bees to take away the pollen. That was maybe a flowery metaphor but it was true. Far better we parted like this than I had an ashtray thrown at my head.

We kept our arms round each other as we slept that night. I did know that I was saying goodbye to a good man. I appreciated that much and it hurt a little. And I also knew that I'd find another man to replace him, whether better or worse. I liked being alone, feeling free for a time but not indefinitely. I had this disaster syndrome where, whenever I lived alone for too long, I'd develop all these fears, these halfwit neuroses about being stalked, getting a disease, being murdered by burglars... I needed loving company. Living alone wasn't natural. Sometimes it felt good but it rarely felt right.

I left after two more days. Joe and I carried my cases outside and looked up at the sky. I felt rain in the air, if not tears. A ladybird crawled down our wall like a bead of paint.

Joe had recruited Max to give us a lift to the train station. We could hear the engine a mile off from his battered orange camper. 'Be Happy' it said on the Union Jack and it cheered us up to get inside the crazy vehicle — it felt like running off to join the circus. Max was wearing a pair of the tightest denim shorts imaginable. The crotch part had faded from blue to white. I couldn't help looking down at his lap as he drove.

We got to the station just before the train pulled in and I was glad we had so little time.

'Keep in touch,' Joe said.

'I will. Good luck with the pub. One day I'll come and get smashed there and make a nuisance of myself.'

'I'll hold you to it.'

We had a hug, some kisses and waved goodbye. Our parting looked banal to all the world but we both felt it.

MAN OF THE NORTH

I t was a bitter morning, two days after Christmas, and Shay started
coughing as soon as he opened his curtains, feeling the draught
from the window pane. His chest ached, but he got around alright
for sixty-three. Wasn't he off to a peace conference near Auschwitz
in the new year and invited to speak at Cambridge at the end of the
month? It was his reward for actively trying to heal the pain of the
past.

He dandered downstairs to the kitchen. The old wooden clothes
horse was warped like it had drifted in from some beach and the
shirts on it still had a salty sweat smell. It was strange, one day living
in damp social housing, the next being the toast of diplomats and
foreign politicos. He saw an image of himself in his suit, slinging back
champagne and prosecco, lifting up dainty morsels in pastry casings.
Some people said he had sold out and the thought of it made him
cringe, but the truth was he'd always had to deal with jealousy.

He got dressed and went out for the paper. It was late morning
but the frost was still whitening the roof tiles and in the sunlight great
plumes of condensation steamed off the houses. It looked like the

whole of the Antrim Road was chain-smoking. In the entry next to his street, the trash was overflowing from the bins like champagne running down the side of a bottle. The pavements were filled with the spoors of Christmas revelry: dope bags, broken bottles, used roaches.

It suddenly struck him that it was Thursday. He had a date that night, no, not a date, as he recalled a flash of blond hair, red lips, marred by a wrinkle or two, but a meeting. Why on earth he'd agreed to meet Anna he didn't know. Of course he'd been at one of those drunken British-Irish Secretariat Christmas dos, where it was easy to make an arrangement only to regret it later.

Inside the corner shop, it felt even colder and the shelves were half-empty as though Marty the owner had given up the pretence of purveying anything more than lotto tickets and fags.

Marty was slumped in a chair behind the counter.

'The head hanging?' Shay asked.

'Busted,' Marty groaned. 'Had about ten pints last night. I need the cure.'

'Have you not heard?' Shay tried to keep a straight face. 'They're doing a suicide special at the garage. A can of petrol and a tow rope. Can't bate it.'

Marty managed a half-hearted laugh and handed Shay his *Irish News*. 'Aye, I'll tell you that right back next time you're in here with a head on you.'

Shay went back to the house and opened the paper. He read it every day, except for a Saturday when he treated himself to *The Irish Times* and *The Guardian*. He had to keep up with things in case journalists would ring him up — Mr Rent-a-Quote he wryly called himself these days.

He scanned through a big article on the Irish border. 'The British border,' he muttered to himself, wondering when everyone would get it. It wasn't the Irish who created that border, it was the British all along. On another page, one of the ex-hunger strikers beamed out, dressed in a smart grey suit fashioned out of one of the blankets from Long Kesh for some memory project or other. Shay cackled out loud, shaking his head, but, fair dos, he granted, he'd been milking the situation himself for years. You had to use the past in this country if you wanted a future. He read on for a while but couldn't settle. He couldn't stop thinking about Anna.

She'd texted him a couple of days ago. It was scarcely credible her fancying him, since she was so much younger — at a guess he'd peg her for late forties. She was also a Protestant, not that she'd remotely divulged that fact but if she had been a Catholic, she would have mentioned a chapel, a Gaelic name, a holy communion or a GAA team, just some sort of Catholic signifier to denote they were of the same tribe, to put each other at ease. All he knew about her was that she worked in the Planning Department of Belfast City Council.

The day started to weigh heavily on him. He couldn't help having expectations about the night ahead. He wasn't sure what scenario scared him more: if she was attracted to him or if she wanted to ask him about his past. To distract himself, he opened his laptop and started jotting down a few bullet points for his Cambridge peace talk. *Bullet* points, he muttered to himself, spotting the irony. The talk was for PHD students in Irish Studies, so he'd have to put on a good show, throw in a few multisyllabic words. As ever, he'd insist his bombs had been the catalyst for peace talks with the Brits. He was honest enough, though, to recognise that history had been kind to him. If he hadn't been let out of prison three years before the hardening of attitudes after 9/11, he might never have been freed. He'd tell Anna all about it tonight.

Shit! Back to Anna again. He got out the ironing board and started pressing his shirts. The sun, after a half-hearted rise, was already sinking down behind the houses. He whistled to himself, excited. He couldn't remember the last time he'd been on a date. Women were interested in his mind, not his body. The philosopher bomber. They looked on him as the last idealist on the planet.

At about six o'clock, he put on his good wool coat and donned his habitual tweed cap. Sometimes the lads teased him for looking like an extra in *Peaky Blinders*, but he needed it for the warmth. He headed out into the darkness. The road was quiet but for a couple of hot hatches passing by, bumping out tunes. Aye, the drug dealers were out and about, already doing their rounds. On the way to the bus stop he passed by an entry, catching sight of a herd of hoodies, white stripes gleaming on their tracksuits. There was something going down, he sensed. He took a step back to look at them. A flash of flame shone out. They were about to set light to the bin.

'Here!' Shay called out.

One of the hoodies dropped the light to the ground in shock at the challenge. He moved out into the slant of the street light, to get a better look at Shay.

'Fuck off, you old cunt. Who do you think you are?' he shouted back, raising his shoulders in anger.

Shay walked on, ignoring him.

'You're nothing!' came another cry. 'Look at me again, I'll brick you, you fucker!'

Shay nervously glanced behind him, thinking he heard a footfall, but the boy had swaggered back into the entry. The boy knew exactly who Shay was, but didn't care. None of the teenagers cared; they were too busy making their own legends. Shay decided against getting the bus as he didn't trust them. Sometimes it was safer to walk than hang round a deserted bus stop.

The pavements were glittering with frost. To his right, as he pressed on into town, the mountains reclined in a black silhouette like a sleeping body and he began to breathe more easily. The next person he came across was a worker outside a hotel throwing salt on the pavement, making sure the well-heeled clients wouldn't slip. Taking care of the rich, mused Shay, rolling his eyes.

A few of the diehard smokers were standing outside Madden's, cursing Christmas for interrupting their diurnal drinking routine.

'Alright, Shay?' called Raymie who was sporting a short-sleeved shirt.

Like a seal pup, thought Shay. Too thick-skinned to feel the cold.

Shay headed straight inside to warm up. The room was wood-pannelled, softly lit, the walls behind the bar plastered with 70s newspaper cuttings of the likes of Bobby Sands and Che Guevara.

The young barman, Liam, poured him a Guinness without asking. Madden's was Shay's home pub and had been for decades. Madden's had wooden stools, no finery, but it was somehow homelier than his housing exec gaff.

'Jesus,' said Raymie, coming back in, bringing with him a huge belch of cold air. 'You missed a cracker in here last night, Shay. We were slaughtered with the drink.'

Shay made out he was listening, but kept turning over the word 'slaughtered' in his mind. It seemed typical to him in this violent little corner of Ireland that 'slaughtered' denoted pleasure.

He looked over at the trad session playing in the corner. A young girl was playing the fiddle, her foot tapping to the tunes. She was wearing a wool dress and her legs were bare. He felt a quick surge of surrogate desire.

Ach, away on, he told himself. Anna wouldn't be interested in the likes of you at sixty-three. Sixty-three and a third, to be exact. Now he was getting older it was as though every month was another sliver of life reclaimed from the jaws of old age. He checked his watch. Five to seven. Normally he was patient. Patience was the trait of every Guinness drinker since you had to wait for it to settle. But tonight he couldn't wait at all. He had already sunk his first pint.

'What are you having, Shay,' offered Raymie, 'apart from a good night? A wee whiskey chaser?'

'No, no,' said Shay. He wanted to keep himself straight for Anna. After all, she might like him, there was no accounting for taste. As his father used to say, 'There's a seat for every arse.'

He was on the first sup of his second Guinness, when the door opened. Anna was smaller than he remembered, prettier than he'd shaped in his memory. It was as if the cold air had freshened her skin, made her shiver with life.

He put his hand up awkwardly to greet her. She smiled and walked over, pulling off her coat.

'What can I get you?'

She looked at his pint. 'Same as you.'

'Guinness it is then,' he said, ordering her a pint, thinking her the type of person who liked to fit in.

'First time I've ever been in here,' she said. Protestant, thought Shay.

'Me too,' said Raymie. 'I first came in here ten years ago and they've never let me out yet!' He slapped the stool next to him in appreciation of his own joke. 'Eh, Liam?'

Shay hastily pointed to a table in the corner.

'Shall we go over here?' he said, moving her away from the bar. Raymie would be all over her, given half a chance. Shay couldn't help notice she was wearing a clinging top, as tight as a second skin.

'So, cheers for coming out,' he said.

'No problem.' She looked uneasily away from his eyes. 'I hope you don't mind me coming. I've heard a lot about you.'

His smile dropped as it was confirmation that all she was after was his story.

'Ah, yes, the bombs. World famous I am. Well, in the North anyway. Or just in Madden's at least.'

'Most feared man in Northern Ireland,' she said, with a defusing laugh.

'I know and look at me,' he said, laughing along with her, pointing out his elderly frame. He'd already clocked her use of 'Northern Ireland' to correct his reference to 'the North'. You never could escape the semantics, the verbal semaphores of the place.

'But the thing is, Anna, I never saw myself as an attacker. My only thought was to protect the community.'

He started telling her about life on the street in Ballymurphy as a young teen. How he watched from his bedroom window the gun battles with the Brits and the way the tracers lit up the darkness as they ricocheted against the walls. The time he'd hoaxed the police by claiming there was a bomb at school, just to pay a teacher back for unjustly caning his best friend. Before his spiel went too dark, he pulled it back with the comedic story of how some kids had found his detonators hidden in their back yard and had thrown one into their fire, bringing a load of soot down. The words were so often spoken they poured out of him now, like it was a well-rehearsed routine, almost a stand-up, well, more of a sit-down but still...

He was vaguely aware of other regulars coming in, the Comanchis, as he called them — Brian the Beard, Fitzy, Head-the-ball from Donegal, but he was so immersed in his story he couldn't break to acknowledge them. He could feel Anna hooked on his words, could see how she observed the twitch of his fingers when he talked about bombs.

'Same again?' He noticed her pint was nearly done.

'No, Shay, it's my turn.'

'Not at all. Sure, I've to get one in for Raymie,' he insisted, getting up.

Raymie turned at the mention of his name. 'Aye, about time, you tight cunt. Here,' he called over to Anna, 'don't be going out with him again. He drinks fast but he orders slow.'

Anna laughed and Raymie put his big arm round Shay protectively.

'I'm only raking you, girl. He'll look after you,' vouched Raymie. 'He's a good lad.'

Shay went back to the table with his pints.

'Cheers,' said Anna, clinking her Guinness against his.

'One of my childhood memories,' he said, 'was how people always looked so happy on booze.'

'You think a lot about the past.'

'I'm paid to,' he thought to himself but stopped himself from saying it.

'So do I,' she said softly. He sensed something was coming. 'I know all about bombing. From the other side. October 23rd 1993.'

He nodded, took a deep gulp of his pint. So this was why she was here. She knew. She knew he'd trained those young bombers up, the ones who had bombed the chip shop that day.

'I was a young nurse on duty in the Royal. Just after lunch, we got word that there had been a huge bomb on the Shankill...'

He felt sick. He wanted to get up and leave, but how could he? Oh, sure, he'd sat on many a panel with victims of his own bombs but he'd been prepared and the public forum of it all had kept back the raw emotion, the recriminations. Without other people around, he felt exposed, frightened even.

She was telling him how she'd helped rush a young boy into theatre with a lacerated leg. The boy was in the final minutes of the golden hour, the hour after injury when he could still be saved. She tried to staunch the bleeding but he'd already lost a lot of blood. She held his hand and his last look was into her eyes. The doctors tried everything, still punching his chest with defibrillators even after he'd long gone. Finally, one of the doctors said, 'Time of death 2.13.'

The boy's Mum had come to the Royal in her slippers as she'd been making lunch when the bomb went off. Anna was the one who had to go out and tell her that her son was dead.

Shay wiped his eyes. It surprised him to well up, but it was the shaking in Anna's voice that broke him. He had his own memories of that afternoon in 1993, rejoicing and yo-hoing with the lads from his cell in Long Kesh at the news of so many Protestants dead — the black jokes flying out thick and fast, 'Oh, we gave the Prods in that chip shop a right 'battering', didn't we?'

That afternoon, she kept wheeling limbs on trolleys to the mortuary. They were draped in bloody sheets and she spoke of how she had to lift dismembered legs, the weight of them hard to balance in her arms. When she finally finished her shift that night, she had a heart-shaped stain on her white tunic.

He listened on, watching her intently, the way she kept her head tilted to one side, as though her blond hair weighed as heavy as gold. It struck him that he was always the one who was being watched and, even though there was pain in her words, it was beautiful for once to listen to someone else.

A day later, she found out that a close friend of hers was missing, presumed dead from the bomb. The DNA tests on what was left of her body later proved it. She lapsed into silence.

Raymie's voice seemed to come from nowhere. 'You two look like you need a pint.' He set some drinks on their table. 'A wee whiskey too.'

'Cheers,' said Shay, realizing Raymie had sensed the darkness between them.

'Whiskey? I'll be on my ear,' smiled Anna.

'Taxi for lightweight!' mock-called Raymie. 'Take it, you'll be grand.'

'Is there no water with it?' Anna asked.

'Water? We don't drink water in here. Sure, fish fuck in water!' replied Raymie, making them all laugh. 'Water, she says,' he continued, pretending to grumble as he headed back to the bar.

Shay knocked back the whiskey in one, feeling it fire up his tongue, waiting for the numbing effect to kick in.

'Anyway, I wanted to talk to you about it,' Anna said apologetically. 'To be honest, I came here and I don't know what I expected.'

'It's fine.'

He wondered if she'd expected him to be contrite. He hadn't set the Shankill bomb, but, still, he'd been complicit in it. If he had set it, he would at least have done a better job of targeting the UVF leaders who met above the chip shop.

'A few months after, I gave up nursing, because of the PTSD,' Anna told him.

'I have PTSD too.'

He could see it as clearly as yesterday. He was on a night mission and had just set a line. As he walked away, a bright light from the circuit on the box flicked on, and he knew it wasn't right, so he quickly ran back and pulled out the det. The box exploded, scorching his hand, throwing up gravel into his face. It could have, should have been much worse. At the time, there had been no fear in him. It was only when it came back to him years later, the burning smell of the plastic in his nostrils, night after night after night, that he realised he had been so close to death.

Anna passed him her whiskey. 'Drink this for me, will you?'

'No bother.' He knocked it back gladly. 'Water of life, they call it. Water of strife more like.'

He told her about how his parents were hard-drinking. At night he'd hear his Mum starting an argument on the whiskey, but his father would always end it with violence. Anna nodded, but made no comment. It occurred to him everything he said sounded like a craven excuse for what he'd become. The only people he could get through to were the ones who had no real memories of the Troubles. As he spoke, he found himself thirsting for her body, an image of himself kneeling in front of her, pulling her down onto his bed and kissing her, tasting her forgiveness.

For that was behind everything he did: to obtain earthly forgiveness for being a freedom fighter, or to some a murderer.

His stomach flipped at the last word. He swallowed hard to keep the Guinness down.

'Look, Shay.' She was pointing towards the door. 'Must be snowing.'

A woman had come in, flakes of pure white settled on her coat. The sight of it calmed him, brought him back to reality.

'I'll need to be away soon,' Anna was saying. 'Don't want to get trapped.'

'Come on, one more for the ditch,' urged Shay. He didn't want her to leave just yet. He hadn't told her the half of it.

'I haven't finished this one yet.'

'Sure it's near dead.'

'It's cool. I'll keep it alive,' she said, swirling her glass round.

He went up for another pint. Raymie had already gone home. He hadn't even noticed him leave. The session had packed up and there were only four other customers left in the bar.

When he came back to Anna, she said, 'You drink too much.'

'I know. No wonder my publisher keeps asking where my memoir is.'

'You're writing a memoir?'

'Yes, but not about me,' he added hastily, in case she thought he was writing his own hagiography, making money on the backs of people he'd killed. 'About the community I grew up in.'

'Funny, isn't it? Me and you sitting here together.'

'I suppose,' he said, 'but I don't care any more about all that Catholic-Protestant carry-on. Sure aren't we all descended from pagans? All I want is for people to come together. That's what I'm about now.'

'Instead of splitting them apart,' finished Anna, then suddenly realised what she'd just said. 'Sorry. I didn't mean literally, I just meant...'

'It's grand, Anna.'

He understood she despised what he'd done, but what would a Prod know about growing up with gun battles, he felt like answering back. It wasn't worth taking the bait. What was it that pastor had once said? It was a quote from some passage in *Corinthians* spoken by Paul — '"To love is not to take offence."'

'That snow's wild out there,' Liam said, as he came over to pick up their empties. 'If you're needing a taxi, I'd better call you one now.'

'Oh, right. Could you order one for me?' asked Anna.

Shay's grasp tightened on his glass. He wished now he'd never entertained those hopes of spending the night with her. His only girl was Guinness. Glynis…Glennis…Gwyneth… He chuckled gently to himself.

'Why are you laughing?'

'Oh, no reason. It's been good to meet you, Anna.'

'I know. It's not often someone understands what it was like back then.'

'No one can understand.'

They put on their coats and he walked her out to the porch of Madden's. The wind had strengthened from earlier. They shivered and watched the diagonal swerves of snow. The old Latin word for Ireland, *Hibernia*, kept repeating itself in his mind. *Hibernia* meaning land of winter. He hoped the taxi wouldn't come because he wanted her company for longer, even if he couldn't find the words.

'Are you not getting a taxi too?' she asked.

'No, I'll walk.' He wanted to save the fare and he was in the mood to walk.

'You're mad. You might fall.'

'I haven't drunk that much. I can hold it. You should see me after eight pints, I'm grand till I get home, then, once I'm through the door I collapse — it's like I've burst!'

Anna laughed.

'Anyway, I never worry about myself. It was always other people I worried about. Like, my Mum died young and I had to worry about all my brothers and sisters.'

The taxi pulled up with a loud toot. Anna bundled herself in and Shay waved her off. He turned away into the driving snow. He didn't know why he'd had to tell her about his mother dying young. It was as if he'd needed sympathy from her, some sort of recognition. He couldn't remember when exactly he'd become so needy. Women didn't like that from men. People didn't like that from people. It was just he was so used to talking to all the academics and peace-facilitators who looked to him for answers, for why he'd become a bomber.

The wind was blowing the snow slantways. In the trees, the

branches were tossing the snow off like bucking broncos. The busy streets had gone quiet and, as he trekked up the Crumlin Road, he started to follow the imprint of a shoe in the snow. Strangely, it was the same size as his own and of a similar stride pattern and he fell into its rhythm. What was that verse again about God, he asked himself, searching his memory. Ah, yes… 'The times when you only saw one set of footprints were the times when I carried you.'

A sudden icy blast sprayed the snow from the roofs down onto the street in front of him. Everyone else is dead but I'm still alive, thought Shay with a surge of triumph. Those who didn't die of their own bombs, had died from the triple D — drink, drugs and depression. Sometimes he wanted to shout out his existence from the rooftops, but other times alone in his house he felt bowed down with survivor's guilt.

He was nearing the part of the Antrim road with the criss-crossing entries. 'You're nothing! You're nothing, you're nothing!'— the boy's shout from earlier kept coming back at him, obliterating him, and he remembered the flash of fire in the black, a fire with a bright dancing heart and a soul colder than snow. He was scared that the boy knew where he lived, might come to him that night. He was sure he could smell a burning in the air.

BOMB DUST

A s the taxi turned into the Shankill, Jake leaned forward, taking it all in. The old flats were being knocked down, the absent outer wall revealing rows of brightly-coloured rooms like a doll's house. A dusty sunlight gauzed the mountains behind. An image of a street grey with bomb dust reared up in his mind, snapshots flickering from one to another — walking home from school in the sunshine, pushing through crowds on a baking Twelfth, trooping behind a hearse in the wind and rain...

'Must be a sale of flags on,' the taxi driver commented sarkily. 'Buy one, get one free.'

A Republican, guessed Jake. You couldn't open your mouth round here without revealing yourself. The slightest inflection, the flick of an eyebrow was enough. But, yes, there were even more flags now: a jubilee gone mad. The murals were crudely drawn, the sign of a society left behind, a society that cared more about message than delivery. The razed ground, where Frizzell's chip shop used to be, lay like a gap from a pulled tooth you felt for with your tongue.

The traffic was slow.

'Why don't you take a left here?' Jake asked.

'It's a one-way,' the taxi driver said. 'This is a taxi, mate, not a fucking helicopter!'

The taxi stopped at the traffic lights outside the Rangers Club. Jake looked up and saw that the green man had fallen over and was lying on his back. It made him smile. A flock of starlings swooped and wheeled above, their ticker-tape wings stuttering through the sun, casting their shadows in a revolving strobe of light and dark across the tarmac.

A woman crossing the road in front peered in at him. He wanted to shrink back but told himself to hold still. There was something about that overbite, the dimpled, cratered chin. The hair was different but it was definitely Mary Brickley, the bitch who'd campaigned to put him out. One of those women who made bullets and got the men to fire them. On this road, nothing went unnoticed. The jungle drums would soon be beating. Tommy, his Dad, had cleared it with the UVF that he could come, but there were plenty like Mary who would still resent his return.

The taxi pulled up outside the house. Tommy was standing at the window watching out for him. It took him an age to come to the door.

'Hurry up,' Jake muttered, feeling exposed, the eyes of the street on his back.

'You're late,' Tommy whispered, shaking hands with him. Tommy's hand still felt reassuringly strong.

'I *am* late' Jake said. 'Seven years late.' It was that long since he'd been home. He wouldn't have come now but for his Dad's illness. 'How are you, Dad?'

'Doing grand, just grand. Tara's been popping in all the time.'

He could hear the whisper of his Dad's breath, like death was already in his lungs, making him speak in hushed tones. Emphysema it was.

'Jesus, it's freez... Baltic in here, Dad.' He caught himself, trying to remember the old slang to make him seem less of a foreigner in his own home.

'Aye, but if it's roasting I can't catch a breath.' There was a plaintiveness in his voice that Jake had never really heard before. Now Jake looked at him, he could see that his big street-brawler's arms had shrunken, his back was bent from nights of coughing.

'That cold you could hang beef in here,' Jake said, trying to make Tommy smile.

A cardboard box full of old letters and memorabilia was sitting on the kitchen table.

'Is that what you want me to go through?'

'That's it,' wheezed Tommy. 'Tara brought it down from the attic. It was always meant for you.'

Sitting there like an unexploded bomb. His grandfather's things. Jake dreaded the thought of looking at them.

'But if you don't want them, you can always pass them on to the Linenhall Library.'

Leafing through the top letters, he noticed a signature on an old certificate, 'Jacob Spencer'. He'd been named after his grandfather, as many boys were round these parts. His grandfather had only ever been kind to him. He liked to ruffle his hair, give him a playful 'bearding' with his rough bristle. When they locked him away, at first Jake had visited him under the impression that 'bad people' had put him in jail, but a few months after his release, Jacob was shot dead by the IRA. It was then that Tommy told Jake what Jacob had done. Only seven years old — surely he was too young to be exposed to all that, but he could hardly blame Tommy for telling him. It was just a matter of time before it all would come out in the playground anyway.

'I'll have a good look tomorrow,' Jake promised.

Tommy nodded as the front door burst open. Still on edge, Jake jumped, but a big 'hello-oh,' bellowed out and Tara breezed in, enwrapping her brother in a big hug.

'Look at you,' she said, feeling his arms. 'You're like a skinned rabbit. Does that English woman of yours not feed you?'

Jacob looked back at her, thinking she hadn't changed much since she'd last visited him, except for a shimmer of lines round her eyes.

'Put that mouldy oul box away,' she went on, 'and I'll pop round for fish and chips.'

'I'll go,' Jake offered but she was so insistent on going he wondered if she was trying to keep him indoors.

'You stay here with Dad,' she told him. 'Sure he hasn't seen you in years.'

He took the box off the table. An attic mustiness clung to the air around it, like the house itself, unchanged, the same old furniture once built for comfort, now sorely in need of an update. The last night he'd spent here, Mary Brickley had told him he was going to be put out of the Shankill, so he'd sat up till dawn with a baseball bat, ready to defend himself. In the morning the police came round to tell him he had a death threat from an active service unit. That same afternoon he caught a flight to Manchester, presented himself to the housing executive and declared himself as homeless.

He went out to the yard for a cigarette. He knew he shouldn't, as his father's illness was caused by smoking. But you couldn't help doing what your predecessors had done. For years he'd wondered if what your family did was encoded in your blood, as if one day hereditary impulses might bubble up in your veins and force you into the same dark acts. The smoke plumed out with his breath as the tightness eased out of him. He was secluded in the walled yard, safe as an anchorite. He'd smoked out here all through his teens till he'd left at twenty-one. Just him and the sky and it had given him respite.

A small child was hooting in another yard as Jake watched a black cat slink across the wall after a spider like it was a lion stalking its prey in the Serengeti. The cat was so absorbed, it didn't give him a second glance. It was funny how in this corner of the world little killers thought of themselves as great warriors.

He went back in and sat down. Tommy sat opposite sucking on

the arm of his glasses like it was a pipe.

'It's so good to see you, Son.' In the ache of his words Jake imagined he was being asked to stay for good now. Tara had told him on the phone that Tommy maybe only had a few more years left in him.

'Aye, but I have a good life over there,' Jake said. He wasn't sure Eva would want to come here and besides he was Jake McMullan now. He'd taken his mother's name in Manchester, changed it by deed poll. Jacob Spencer was no part of him now.

'Your wee mate, Paul, said he'd be in the Rangers tonight. Everyone wants to see you.'

Jake could feel the world suck him in. He already knew he'd have to keep coming back. He hated himself for thinking it, but he half-hoped that his Dad would die in his sleep peacefully by the end of the year.

His mobile rang. It was Eva and he ran up to his old room to take it.

'Everything's great,' he told her, remembering her thighs scissoring his hips the previous night and the tingles in his body afterwards, spent and wrung-out, holding her in his arms. As he talked, he ran his fingers down the wall of his old room, feeling for the holes of the nails that had secured the posters of his childhood. The old Man U poster. It seemed crazy but the only reason he'd gone to Manchester was because he loved the football team.

Downstairs, he could hear his father's ragged cough, a nettle-bed of scratches for air. He'd get used to the sound in time, he told himself.

After tea, Jake decided to go to the Rangers after all.

'Good on you,' Tommy said.

'Aren't you going to stay and chat with Dad?' Tara's voice was sharp and Jake finished the sentence for her in his own head, 'after seven years away.'

'Not at all. Let him go out and have some fun with Paul. Did you know he works for Addiction NI now?'

'Aye, well, there are enough addicts in the Rangers for him to practise on,' Jake laughed, ignoring the hint that Paul might be able to fix him up with a job.

Outside, the brightness was starting to seep out of the sky. The wind was getting up in a way that made the body clench, signalling that snow was on its way.

Jake was heading through the maze of side streets but stopped and drew in his breath. A baby was hanging out of an open window! Looking more closely he realised it was just a doll, bent over, its head on the window sill. He laughed in relief, though it had nearly given him a heart attack. He inwardly applauded the trompe l'oeil of the kids who'd staged it. Sure, where else in the world would you see it?

He passed the huge Presbyterian church he'd attended as a child with his grandfather. Those massive sandstone bricks the colour of yellow-grey slush, the surrounding hedge cut back, the branches sharp as stakes. A daffodil was peeping its bright face through the church gate like it was behind prison bars. The sight of it reminded Jake that the funeral of his grandfather was the last day he'd stepped inside. Tommy had always described that day's service as interminable, joking that the only thing he'd prayed for was a shorter sermon.

Up ahead the Rangers looked warm, lights glowing behind the misted windows. Two guys were standing outside smoking, collars up. One of them wore shoes with upturned toes, radiating cockiness.

'Jacob Spencer,' he said to the other, making sure Jake could hear.

Jake's step faltered. He didn't even recognise them, but they knew him. Talking *about* him before they talked *to* him. It felt like judgment. Condemnation. Or maybe it was approval as his grandfather to this day was still revered by some as some kind of Ulster hero.

He realised he wasn't ready to go in. He couldn't take the scrutiny. Instead, he veered to the left, taking the opportunity of the supine green man on the traffic lights to cross the road. He turned direction swiftly towards the town, towards the half-demolished flats and the old rusted pipes on each floor sticking out like roots. To his right, a road sloped down to the peace wall. A gritter rumbled past, sowing lines of salt.

The reason he'd had to leave the Shankill was because he'd been talking at meetings on the other side of the peace wall, telling them he wanted to live in a drug-free, fearless community. Some of the UVF objected to him talking to Sinn Féin, jealous of his fame. 'So what if I talk to them?' he'd retorted. 'I'm only doing what you've been doing the past twenty years behind closed doors.' 'But they're using you for your name,' they argued, and he had to admit it was true. The grandson of a notorious UVF killer was media gold dust to Sinn Féin.

Lie low for a bit, Tommy had said at the time, let the dust settle. But the trouble was the dust took too long to settle in these parts; even over the graves it still wouldn't settle.

Wasn't it all mad, he thought to himself. He'd taken on his mother's name, McMullan, only to find out weeks later from a woman of the same name that the McMullans had been one of the most ferocious Scottish clans, famous for cutting the ears off their victims. How about that for irony?

Downhill ahead of him the city lay, a bowl of neon lights like a big bright nightclub. A girl hurried past him, telling friends on her smartphone she was on her way. A slab of blue neon illuminated her cheek. Above, the darkening sky was spraying tiny flakes of snow like it was promising a night of cocaine and speed.

He turned to his right, intuitively aware of where he was going.

He had never been there, only visualised the spot as a child and he'd tried not to think of it these past seven years. But now he wanted to see it. The red brick houses looked out onto the grey razor-wired peace wall, some of the windows boarded up as though erasing the view from sight. No man's land was a quiet stony field of weeds and brambles and dandelion leaves. It was so cold but as he walked on his body began to burn with tribal fear. Three times he had been to the Falls to talk about peace; he knew St Mary's, the Cultúrlann, An Cúpla Focal, but he'd never walked there alone.

Much to his surprise the gate on North Howard Street was wide open. He guessed he'd made it across just in time. It was deserted. All the tourists had long since fled back to the city bars and hotels, and no one else would be mad enough to cross by foot after dark.

Suddenly his mobile rang. In the shelter of the peace wall it was piercing. He checked it, smearing a few snowflakes off its face. Paul. One missed call from Tommy too. Keeping tabs on him, oh, aye, the eyes were always on you in this country.

He walked onto the Falls Road, feeling much safer in the churn and spray of passing traffic. Past the International Wall with its murals and legends, its poster-boy hunger strikers. He kept walking further up the Falls, the green trim of the closed shops almost glowing. Divis Flats at his back as tall as a Celtic standing stone. The paving stones were moon-white now, showing him the way. He kept seeing his grandfather's photo in his head, the prison mugshot that had adorned every newspaper for years. Jake had looked at it a thousand times, seen the same blue, shallow-lidded eyes, praying that he didn't look the same. His own smile, that was a pure McMullan smile and the nature of a being was in the smile, not in the eyes. The long hair and the sideburns from the seventies... Jake had kept his hair short so he'd never look like him. Still, he often caught people observing him closely, wondering if the beast lurked in him too.

He came to the street sign, Springfield Road / *Bóthar Chluanaí*. *Bóthar Chluanaí*, he repeated, mocking the Irish because old habits died hard with him. And he saw it ahead, Crocus Street, the quiet corner where in 1975 his grandfather and his two mates had picked up that Catholic boy in their black taxi, offering him a lift. *Why did you have to do it?* he asked the sky, the white cloud lying over the blackness, stifling out the stars. Oh, it was easy to say it was a tit-for-tat — his grandfather's close friend was blown up in his own car — but it wasn't a cold-blooded execution. It was random, frenzied hatred, an innocent boy...

After Jacob Spencer and his team had picked the teenager up, they brought him to a shooting shed on the outskirts of Woodvale. But they didn't shoot him. They tied him up. They took out boning knives and hatchets. Seventy-eight separate wounds were found on the teenager's body.

His grandfather took to religion in prison, was born again, but it was too late.

Jake shivered in the wind that hurled flinty fragments of ice into his face. The snow shifted beneath his feet, pitching him onto the ground. *Born again?* he cried out. *That boy never got a chance to be born again, did he? Why did you ever come here? Why did you take my name away from me? I never had a chance with this name. Jacob, Jake, Jakey, Spencer, Spense, suspense, Jacko, Kajob, bake job, bastard, bastard, bastard, fucking cunt! FOR I THE LORD YOUR GOD, AM A JEALOUS GOD, VISITING THE INIQUITY OF THE FATHERS ON THE CHILDREN, ON THE THIRD AND FOURTH GENERATIONS OF—*

'Hey!'

A shout cut across him.

He looked up at a group of teens moving in to surround him. He could feel the fear creeping into his stomach. What was he doing here, flat-out in the wet snow? Surely they would guess he was someone in the wrong part of town. A head like a dark eclipse against the corona of streetlight hovered above him. He instinctively put his hand up in defence.

'Are you alright, mate?' A teenage boy was speaking softly through his scarf. Jake began to make him out through the streetlight. The boy's short hair was crusted with snow, his ears beetroot from the raw wind. He couldn't have been more than sixteen, had the hard, streetwise expression of someone who'd been kicked by life.

'Homeless he is, or mental,' a girl's voice said.

'He's hurt.'

'Call him an ambulance.'

'No, no,' Jake mumbled. He tried to get up to his feet but realised his legs were so cold he couldn't move.

'Here, help him up,' the boy said to a friend and Jake felt the hook of their arms, pulling him up, his feet slipping on the snow, then finding their grip.

'Where do you live?' someone asked.

Jake bolted at the question, his hand sliding against the red bricks of Crocus Street.

'Wait. Do you need a taxi, friend?' the boy called out.

Jake stumbled away, then realised there was no one following. He turned and looked back.

'Thank you!' he shouted, but they were gone.

An old phrase from the Bible came back to him — *Be kind to strangers for they might be angels unawares.* He remembered how his grandfather had told him, only days before they shot him, that early Christians believed the highest part of the heavens was made of fire for all light came from it. The thought came to his mind: he would throw out that box, slough off that past for ever. He walked home through the streets luminiferous with white snowdust, back to the Shankill.

LIFESTYLE CHOICE 10MG

Sometimes you think you're going to get back into the swing of things, when life swings right back at you. It was six months after my back operation and I'd thrown out the painkillers and was feeling so much better I moved into a new house with a brand new housemate. I also started a six-month contract at the examinations board. I thought maybe I could meet a guy but I'd forgotten that admin offices are so populated by females they're practically like girls' schools. At any rate, now I was fit and healthy I could at least make some friends.

By my second week in the office, I hadn't made any friends. My boss, Laura, was a bottle brunette who was loud and gesticulative— sometimes it looked like she wanted to karate-chop you. There was one other long-term inmate, Marie-Louise, who had a phone permanently clamped to her head like a handle and lipstick that bright you couldn't keep your eyes off her lips, though to be fair the conversation that emitted from them didn't warrant the same attention. Marie-Louise was exceedingly deferential to Laura, as if scared she would suddenly make some fatal mistake—it was more as if she was a junior surgeon than an office worker. That was the real problem with our office. Every time you turned, Laura was watching you.

Apart from myself, there was one other temp, Hannah. She was two years younger than me and married. Marie-Louise, who never tired of talking about her aspiring actress daughter, Seaneen, kept making presumptuous hints about it being time Hannah had kids. I liked Hannah but she was so efficient she made me look bad.

I thought to myself, how the hell am I going to last six months? When I arrived home at the end of that week, I wasn't sure if the aches and pains in my back were physical or spiritual, but I definitely regretted throwing out the Tramadol. I decisively rapped on my house-mate Paddy's door.

'Do you have any painkillers?'

'Yep, these are the biz, Alice,' he said, ushering me in and opening a drawer. 'These babies will smooth you out real sweet.'

Paddy's not into much more than a bit of dope and the odd coke-insufflation, but that's the thing about drugs, when people talk about them they tend to act like a cool-ass dealer from the Bronx.

I walked out with them in my hand. Co-codamol 30.

I banged a couple the next morning for breakfast. By the time I got to work, I felt very chilled. I could actually feel this low-level smile on my face and, what was more, I was functioning. Though to be fair, the job of stuffing letters into envelopes could have been accomplished by a chimp. But the main point was that the morning was speeding along nicely.

In the afternoon, Laura sent me to the photocopier and I dallied somewhat, enjoying being out of the office. After fifteen minutes, she came out to find me, not looking best pleased.

'It was only a few pages, Alice,' she snapped. 'It's not the entire phone book.'

The next morning I went to the doctor's about my back. One of the great things about Northern Ireland is that prescriptions are free on account of us having been so troubled by the Troubles. He prescribed me some Butrans, a pain patch I'd used before for my back. I had to sign for them at the front desk as they're a controlled drug. I then ran round to Boots with the script and it was like Fort Knox — it took about ten minutes for the safe to open. Anyway, I slapped on the patch and headed to the bus stop. It was already nine-thirty and I should have phoned Laura but Belfast is the Bermuda Triangle for buses — you're lucky if they turn up at all. By the time the bus pulled up, my stress rate was starting to go through the roof.

'May I see proof of your doctor's appointment?' Laura asked straight away. It was hard not to take the lack of trust personally but it was the culture of the place. That very week, the building was being installed with clocking-in cards, as the managers were concerned the staff weren't putting in a full day's work. During the coffee break, Laura took us over to the machine to show us how it worked.

'Jesus, it's like we're wage slaves back in the twentieth century,' I whispered to the others.

'Here, look what Seaneen had for dinner at the theatre awards,' buzzed in Marie-Louise, showing us poorly paid temps living on baked beans a Facebook photo of delicious steak and courgette parcels. Marie-Louise was the sort of person who would show it to a famine victim.

By the afternoon, I'd popped another couple of Co-codamols and the slow-release Butrans was beginning to kick in. I bore in mind the fact that Laura had objected to my slowness the previous day so I picked up the pace. I was packing the envelopes at a fair old speed, enjoying the admiring murmurs of Hannah, when Laura called out, 'Slow down there, Alice.' She wasn't amused. I guessed she saw it as showing up how easy and menial all our jobs were. She came over to my desk, eyed my envelopes suspiciously, and promptly sent me off to the guillotine.

'Who, am I, Marie Antoinette?' I couldn't help quipping and Hannah laughed, precipitating a frown from Laura.

When I returned, the mood in the office was sombre. Laura pointed out that one of my envelopes hadn't been properly adhesed. She surveyed the edges of the guillotined pages with as much assiduity as if she was applying a spirit level to them. I returned to filling the envelopes at the glacial pace more suited to my chilled, medicated state. Marie-Louise's eyelashes fluttered hectically like nervous moths when Laura spoke. I was tempted to pop a Co-codamol into her Earl Grey that break-time just to help her relax.

Hannah's envelopes were perfect. She was almost too good to be true, but I often noticed that when she held a pen her fingers were tense and white.

That weekend, I had a great time. I discovered you couldn't get a hangover on Butrans as your head was already pre-medicated when you woke up the next morning. Paddy kindly gave me a new painkiller, Lyrica, which being the cool dude he was, he called 'bud'. I gave him a couple of tins of tuna in return. Lyrica – it was a poetic name for a little red and white pill. I read the blurb inside and it was an epilepsy drug used in low-level doses for pain. When I took it, it was mad because the room literally lit up.

Monday morning, I clocked in quite happily at work. I was glad to see Laura was smiling.

'We saw you on TV,' she smirked.

It came back to me how over the weekend I'd met up with some friends who were at an anti-Donald Trump rally. I'd wandered into a cameraman's periphery and had inadvertently appeared on the local news. It transpired that I was the talk of the building, since there was never much gossip around. I didn't particularly mind being cast in the role of office revolutionary, even though I was more anti-Trump's candy floss hair than his policies. A couple of supervisors came over to chat to me about the rally at the break and I sensed that Laura's attempts to defame me as a troublemaker had actually elevated me. Marie-Louise was totally jealous. She kept trying to divert the limelight by showing everyone Seaneen's promo shots in her underwear.

That week, I often caught Laura looking at me thoughtfully. She kept pinching her chin like there was some neuropathic pain she couldn't quite locate. I would have offered her a pill, but I don't think she would have appreciated it. She was probably on some hormone pills herself as the window at her back kept lighting up the peachy menopausal fuzz on her cheeks. It reminded me of the white fur on the red bricks in our run-down part of town.

For February, the days were sunny. As I walked home after work through the docklands, there was a soul-warming glow before the blue lid of evening closed on the day. I always passed by a huge sign, belonging to an engineering company, that advertised 'Radiant Works'. I hadn't a clue what they were but I would have loved to be known for radiant works myself.

Paddy rapped on my door again one night.

'Have some OxyNorm,' he said, pushing another package into my hands. 'It's little brother to OxyContin — hillbilly heroin they call it in the States.'

He quickly slipped back into his room, as if he'd just done a street deal. I hadn't asked him for anything more but his day job was a delivery driver, so I guessed he just enjoyed delivering things.

The following week, I was chatting to another supervisor in the corridor who kept rubbing her stiff neck. 'Here,' I said, offering her a

Co-codamol.

'Thanks,' she replied, reluctantly taking it, 'But I'm already on Tramadol.'

It's weird. Once you're on drugs, you find out nearly everyone else is on drugs.

'Well, try some Lyrica instead. Or an OxyNorm. Gets you through your day great.'

She turned them down swiftly and left.

Later, not only Laura, but everyone was looking at me and I began to worry if the supervisor had said anything. I'd only given her a Co-codamol, not a truth serum!

That afternoon, we temps were farmed out to other offices, to help with collating exam papers. I hadn't been out the office long when Laura came to find me.

'Could I borrow my girl back, please?' she asked the supervisor. I felt like a Polynesian slave.

She took me into an empty office and we sat down.

'Here's your one month assessment form,' she said, passing it across.

I read it. It was abysmal. From scores out of five, I scored one or two. I was awarded a generous three for my interaction with colleagues.

'Are you sacking me, Laura?'

'No, I have no grounds to,' she said. 'But I'm going to temporarily transfer your skills next door.'

And so began a new era in the building. I was shown to a computer facing a blank wall. I had to transfer information into a database. Just one simple task all day that was evidently deemed within my capabilities. The boss, Tony, was very cocky and he liked everyone else to be quiet so he could talk and crack jokes. His screensaver actually said 'Mute All', to make sure we got the message. He was bald with wavy whiffs of hair. Funnily enough, his full name was Tony O'Hare – Tony No'Hair, I silently designated him. What was it with this building? The men had too little hair, the women too much. In spite of him, life passed smoothly — well, not everything passed smoothly. I was horribly bunged up on the meds. I lived on a diet of prune juice and syrup of figs.

I often met up with Hannah in the canteen. One lunch time, Marie-Louise broke the news about Seaneen's pregnancy and triumphantly showed us the ultrasound. It was weird because the baby's head didn't look attached to its body, but I didn't dare point it out. From a nearby table, Laura shouted over, 'You're next, Hannah!'

Hannah smiled back in a watery way.

'They don't understand,' she told me, lowering her voice. 'I had cancer. I had a hysterectomy when I was only twenty-five. Why does everyone just assume you can have children?'

I suddenly felt close to her. She didn't want to tell them. She didn't want their pity and I understood that. Everyone in that building had the same aspirations. To have a partner, babies, a mortgage, a car. Hannah would have been the same only her body wouldn't let her. In my case, it was my mind.

One morning, Tony came in brandishing a statuette he'd won the previous night for Best Team Leader.

'Yesss, I'm the best!' he crowed.

As soon as Laura came in, he lifted his award. 'You might win one of these bad boys yourself next year.'

'I doubt it,' said Laura.

'I doubt it too,' he said cruelly. 'Only the best get these.'

It was strange — much as I disliked her I still didn't want to see her demeaned by Tony.

Tony was rubbing his award with his sleeve. 'It's dirty. Where can I clean it?'

'The toilet?' I suggested, and Laura laughed gratefully.

I turned back to the wall, thinking we all needed an award for working here. Things were so bad, I even missed hearing about Seaneen. I got to thinking, what the hell was I doing, parked there like I was in the dunce's corner. Fuck sake, I was juiced up to the eyeballs on meds like I was in some lunatic asylum. It wasn't just my job either. At home, I shared with a man who gave me meds and who dwelt on such topics as how to smuggle a kilo of dope up your arse into prison or how to sniff petrol out of a scrambler.

It was insane — I was on more painkillers than after my back operation! My inventory in the past month had included:

Co-codamol 30mg
Dihydrocodeine 30mg
Butrans 10mg
Lyrica 75mg
OxyNorm 10mg
Zamadol 100mg slow release (my own private Xanadu)
Amitriptyline 30mg (it was a trip alright)

I'd ingested more in the past weeks than Prince, or even Elvis. I would be seriously damaging myself at this rate, and all just to survive a meaningless job of never-ending data. It wasn't even as meaningful as meaningless, it was just a fictitious task invented to keep me out of Laura's hair. I was thirty now and I had to get a move on. My options were obvious: I could clear my head of meds, move into a flat on my own and start applying for something I was really interested in, like a job in the arts.

I stripped the pain patch off my arm. Underneath, my skin was pink and inflamed. When I got up from my desk, Tony was inspecting the new office hoover.

'There's a new sucker coming to work here,' he joked.

'And another one bites the dust,' I chipped in, leaving the room.

I went next door into Laura's. Laura wasn't there, but Hannah seemed happy to see me.

'She's back!' exclaimed Marie-Louise.

'Too right,' I said, jumping into Laura's chair and spinning round in it.

Marie-Louise and Hannah were still laughing when Laura came back. She clearly longed to bite my head off for sitting in her chair, but before she could say anything, I jumped up. 'Could I have a word with you outside, Laura?'

We walked into the corridor. I took a deep breath.

'You've probably noticed I'm not happy here. I'd like to leave.'

'Okay, Alice. Fine,' Laura nodded. 'When were you thinking of going?'

'Today.'

She laughed. I didn't know if it was my going that amused her or my desire for immediate release.

'You're right,' she said, calculating quickly. 'Life is too short. I'll phone recruitment. They can pay you up to the end of the week and you can leave today.'

'Thanks.'

She shook my hand before she went back in and looked at me with curiosity. 'Everyone will be heart-jealous of you going, you know,' she admitted. 'They'll miss you. In some ways, you were a ray of light in here.'

I walked back into Tony's office, feeling happy, for the first time in a month *really* feeling. I couldn't believe she'd thought of me as a ray of light. Of course, it wasn't a ray that she remotely liked shining near her, but nevertheless...

A little later, I was sitting at the computer when Hannah and Marie-Louise bounced up.

'We heard you're going,' Hannah said.

Marie-Louise went to kiss me and I ended up awkwardly missing her cheek and planting a full smacker on her crimson-coated
lips.

At six o'clock, I left the building with the rest of the exodus. The
clouds in the sky were full of orange fiery passion. There wasn't even
a ghost of an ache in my body. I skipped across the road to celebrate
my freedom, making a car brake. I turned and it was Laura, her
face reddening, firing out so many curses the spittle flew out of her
mouth like windscreen washer. I guessed she was regretting that bit
about the ray of light—it must have just slipped out in the relief of
my leaving. I gave her a cheery wave. The streetlights began to shine
like pink gemstones, and I already was planning where I could take
my light to next.

NIGHT HAZE

It was two o'clock when Rachel walked into the Merchant, the nerves rising in her. She pulled the belt of her jacket in tighter. The foyer was prismed with stain-glassed light. Her grandfather had worked in this building when it was a bank—now it was a hotel, it was still raking in the money. And, today, money was why she was here too.

Most of the men did a double-take at her, and some of the women too, which gave her a rush of confidence. She was wearing a short black dress and a jacket she'd originally thought had been black in the shop mirrors but actually turned out to be dark purple in daylight.

She went through to the café/bar. There were a few men in suits sitting alone at tables, but one in particular raised his face to her in expectation. He was about forty, had bright blue eyes and a vivid tie, loosely knotted. He stood up and offered his hand.

'Sean Hilton. And you must be Mia.'

'I am,' she smiled.

'Have a seat,' he said, all urbane charm. 'What will you have to drink?'

She ordered a coffee. She could have done with a real drink, but she had to be professional.

'So, you're twenty-four,' said Sean, perusing her CV. 'I see you're university-educated, you speak French and Spanish...'

'Si, señor,' she said, to make him laugh.

Now she'd time to look at him, she observed that his right eye was slightly larger and more hooded than the other. He made her think of a gem specialist who weighed up the worth of everything through one solitary eye.

'So, Sean, what exactly does being an escort entail?'

A week ago she'd been sitting on her bed, looking for office jobs in the paper. Her last temping job had ended and she wasn't particularly adept with computers, so the most she could hope for was another position as a low-paid dogsbody. Nobody cared for her degree. All they wanted was technocrats. She scanned the page and spotted the advert for escorts. She immediately dismissed it and then went back to it, enticed, and thought, fuck it. If the world didn't want her mind, why couldn't she use her looks instead?

There was a knock on her door. It was Stephen, her housemate.

'You haven't got the oil money, have you?' he asked.

She didn't have it and she apologised, feeling bad. She cringed inwardly at the prospect of asking her parents. She was always asking for money and they in turn asked her when she'd be self-sufficient.

She went back into her room. The rain was on her window, making quick spitting sounds like the second hand on a clock. She grabbed up the paper again, looking excitedly at the ad. She had slept with about ten men already in her life just for fun and, to be honest, usually after copious amounts of alcohol. The only boyfriend she'd ever loved had broken up with her, so she was completely free.

The rain got heavier, weaving in plaits down the windowpane. Outside, the ancient gutters drooped in lopsided smiles. She thought of the shame if anyone found out. Yet, how would they ever know? All you had to do was give a false name. A bigger hurdle was that she thought of herself as a feminist, which didn't exactly equate to selling yourself to men. However, you could always tell yourself that you were taking control of your body and selling it as a commodity, in exactly the same way you'd sell out your brain to a paltry, mind-numbing admin job.

She could talk herself in and out of it all day, but the bottom line was she needed one hundred and fifty pounds for Stephen.

She picked up her mobile and rang the number.

'You'll escort businessmen who are over for a night in Belfast to restaurants, to the opera, to the Waterfront...,' Sean explained. 'Wherever they want to go, you'll accompany them.'

'This basically means I have sex with them, doesn't it?' she said, cutting to the chase.

'Well, that's entirely up to you.' He selected his words carefully. 'What two adults do is none of my business. You are paid merely to provide the client with company.'

'I'm not sure anyone'd pay two hundred quid for conversation— well, not unless it's as witty as Oscar Wilde.'

'You'd be surprised what clients want,' he said archly, not to be drawn. 'Occasionally they may be female. Would you have any objections to that?'

'None.'

'Good,' he smiled. He picked up the photo of her. 'This is a cute photo. But we need something frankly a bit sexier. Could you email us one?'

'No problem.'

He scribbled a quick note, the pen tucked tightly between his thumb and fist.

'Yes. I think we'd definitely like you in our portfolio. You're very attractive, your height, your complexion…'

'Really?' she said, blushing.

'Yes, though, to be honest, you are a bit on the skinny side.'

Her face dropped.

'Don't be insulted,' he said quickly, his face dropping too. 'Some men prefer that. We're here to cater for all tastes. Look, I'll phone you tomorrow and we can talk some more, okay?'

She walked out into Waring Street. It was early September and the afternoon was diaphanous with sunlight and softly zipping insects. The air was windless; even the dust was sleeping. She decided to walk home to save the bus fare in spite of her heels. And, she had to admit, she was enjoying how men looked at her in the street. Normally she schlubbed round the city in jeans. A boy of eighteen or nineteen grinned at her. He was gleamingly clad in white skinny jeans and a white shirt in spite of the grime of the city. Like an urban angel, she thought. A gold chain fell around his neck like a slipped halo and she longed for him.

An elegant woman was sitting outside The Northern Whig with a glass of wine at her lips, like she was breathing in the scent of a dark red rose. Rachel looked at her with envy, wishing she could spend the afternoon drinking. She calculated how quickly she could pay off her debts at two hundred pounds a night. She really prayed that Sean would phone, but then realised the word 'pray' was totally inappropriate for what she was planning to do. She'd walked through a moral door when she'd gone in to see him.

At home, there was a letter sitting on the mantelpiece. It was from the landlord, informing her she was late with her rent and he required it ASAP. She went through to the kitchen. Her shelf in the fridge was empty except for a couple of Babybel and a punnet of plums. There was one can of lager toppled over at the back and she lifted it out and snapped it open. The ring pull gave a sigh of released pressure and she glugged the lager down needily. A bluebottle was head-banging the kitchen window. She opened the upper window but it couldn't seem to find its way out.

God, an escort! Sean had liked her, she was sure of it, and she had to admit it was flattering to have her looks validated, but she couldn't quite believe she was going through with it. She bit into a plum. The juice flooded out of its bright yellow skin. It tasted like the whole of that summer's sunshine was distilled in its flesh.

It was barely a week before she was offered her first client. Lucy, the girlfriend of Sean's business partner, called her with the details.

The following evening, she waited outside Ox. A taxi pulled up and a large man wearing a dark suit in his early fifties stepped out. Her first thought was that he was overweight and bald but he had such a confident smile she was already won over.

His name was John Woolf. She'd googled him and found out he was a property developer from Cheltenham. They took a candle-lit table and he didn't waste time in ordering an array of dishes, which made her guess he'd been at Ox many times before with escorts. Or perhaps that was unfair and he'd been there with business clients.

'So, what do you do, Mia?'

'I work in computers.'

'What type of computers?' he asked.

'Oh...er...office...databases, spreadsheets.'

He laughed out loud and mimicked her vagueness. 'Er...er...if you're going to lie to your clients you should really make sure you think it out first.'

'God, yeah,' she said embarrassed. 'The truth is I'm terrible with computers. I'm actually unemployed.'

'And do you have a boyfriend? Remember, if you tell me you're hitched with six kids, I'll not believe you now.'

'No, no man. I'm totally free.'

He told her all about his wife, and his girlfriend who worked for him. His girlfriend had been an escort when they'd met. Though he talked, he still ate quickly like he was on the clock.

'So how many clients have you had?' he asked.

She hesitated but, as he'd already called her out on a lie, truth seemed the better option.

'You're my first,' she said, thinking she sounded like a virgin.

'Wow,' he said, grinning. He seemed honoured.

On one of the plates, there were marinated strips of raw beef, oozing blood. She ate one and it melted in her mouth like a kiss. She tried not to drink too much wine, reminding herself to stay in control, but every time he looked at her lips, she couldn't help lifting her glass to them self-consciously.

'I have a proposition for you,' he said, leaving it hang in the air.

'Go ahead, John.'

'Why don't you come to Cheltenham and work for me in my office?'

'You're kidding.'

He reached out and felt the lapel of her jacket. 'You look good in this but you would look amazing in Nicole Farhi. I can buy you that. And you'll work when you want. Go on, what have you got to lose?'

She had an image of belonging to him. The dare appealed to her but all her soul screamed against it. 'I'm not sure.'

The thrill of the deal was in his eyes. 'Go on, I dare you.'

She looked away uncomfortably. At that exact moment, a young guy at the table behind them smiled at her quizzically, as if to ask what the hell she was doing with this old man.

'Ah,' said John. 'Too scared. I thought so. But if you ever change your mind...'

He passed her his card.

They left Ox and got a taxi to Bullit. He held her hand during the short trip and bantered with the driver. It was only when walking into the lobby that he fell quiet and she finally felt like an escort, rather than a date.

His room was large, airy and impersonal. She realised in its quietness she was drunker than she'd thought. He threw his keycard onto the table and kissed her. She wondered if she should ask him what he would like. All she was going by was what she'd seen on TV where prostitutes appear confident and vampish, but, as she'd confessed it was her first time, it seemed foolish to put on an act.

They eyed one another nervously, each waiting for the other's move. He started taking off his clothes, folding them neatly on the chair. She mirrored what he was doing. It felt clinical, not lustful. It was exactly what it was, a transaction. She had once read about Van Gogh and what he called his 'hygienic excursions' to the brothel.

But, then, she saw there was something about his body; its fleshiness was surprisingly taut and the white hairs on his chest glimmered in his honey skin. She was so pale herself, she couldn't resist darker shades of skin and the raw scent of him drew her in like a mosquito.

Naked, she moved towards him. He pushed her onto the bed and leapt on top of her, spinning over so that she was on top. He moaned and kept smacking her on the buttocks with his hand, his groans rising. She groaned too, at first to echo him, then with desire. He stopped a second and expertly slipped on a condom, then clasped her tight to him. In a matter of minutes, he had come, his beating, heaving heart pressed fast against hers.

She rolled out from under him and went to the bathroom. She had a pee, then washed her hands. The light was harsh, highlighting the curves and shadows of her face. She couldn't help looking at herself, thinking she'd somehow changed. The basin was pure white like a pumice stone. She had the strange sensation that she was dipping her fingers into a font of holy water.She could hear the jingle of his keys coming from the room, the soft shimmy of material against skin and realised he was already getting dressed. The man's on a mission, she thought to herself, hurrying through to him. He was already phoning the lobby for a taxi. So that's how you get to be a million-aire, she smiled to herself.

It was about eleven when they arrived at the casino.

'Just after university, I applied for a job to be a croupier in London,' she told him.

'And?'

'Unfortunately, my maths weren't as quick as my words,' she grinned.

She'd almost forgotten that at one time she'd been attracted to glitz and riches. A succession of low-paid jobs made you forget what was possible, but tonight she was enjoying herself beside this strong, barrel-chested man. He bought her a hundred pounds worth of chips and led her to an empty blackjack table.

'You play, I'll watch,' he said, looking on proudly like a father watching his child have fun in a play park. 'Whatever you win, you keep. The last girl I brought here won two hundred. Let's just see if you can do any better.'

She won the first couple of hands. He got interested, his eyes started to glitter and she knew he was turned on by winners. She lost the next hand, then another, and found herself on a losing streak. In no time, she was down to fifty pounds.

'That'll do,' she said, not wanting to lose the lot.

'Fine by me' said John. He looked tired now. As they left, his walk was slower. It was as if the magic spell had ended at the tick of midnight. He looked every one of his fifty plus years.

He gave her a rough kiss outside and said goodnight. It was rain-ing now. He gave her a tenner for her taxi, then got in the taxi behind. At the end of the road, the two taxis turned in opposite directions.

She wished she'd done better on the blackjack, partly for the money, but also to have impressed him. Even more than that, she wished she'd proved to herself she could be a winner. She checked that she still had his card. She couldn't stop thinking about him. Every inch of her smelled of him.

She stopped the taxi about five minutes from her house. It was her habit to try and save a couple of pounds off her fare, but she hadn't even noticed the weather. As she walked into her street, a big squall came on, bringing heavy rain. A tree branch flicked a plume of water down the back of her neck and puddles ambushed her feet, as if the weather was playing a prank on her; as if it was putting her back in her place for outreaching herself tonight. But, no matter how hard it tried, it couldn't wash the memories of the night away.

'So, how was the Woolf?' Sean asked when he phoned her a few days later.

'Big and bad,' laughed Mia.

'Did he give you extra?' he checked.

She told him about her gambling fund. She'd already received her two hundred pounds from Lucy the previous day when she'd met her at Central Station.

'But did he ask you to leave the agency?' pressed Sean.

She was surprised he knew, but he explained that John Woolf had approached a previous escort with the same proposition.

'If you go, we'd need him to pay a severance fee,' he said, sounding severe. 'You do understand, we'd never let you go otherwise.'

It struck her that her body belonged to Sean. It was odd. She'd never even signed a form.

'Don't worry,' she reassured him. 'I turned him down.'

'Great,' said Sean. 'We've a lot more clients for you. Lucy will give you a buzz soon.'

She checked herself in the mirror above the mantelpiece but it was always hard to see anything in their crepuscular house. She glanced out the window again but still no sign of her taxi.

'Another blind date tonight?' Stephen asked.

'Yep.'

'He'd have to be blind not to like you,' he joked.

He was happy with her because she'd paid him the oil money out of her earnings. After tonight, she'd have the rent for her landlord too. She'd also buy some more silk underwear and stockings. She'd always believed that this kind of clichéd bedroom paraphernalia was just for the sake of attracting men, but it was strange. As soon as she felt the silk against her, she immediately wanted sex.

Outside, the sky was a neon cocktail of light. Above the mountains was a measure of crème de menthe, followed by orange and topped by pink syrup. Rachel, her mood soaring, longed to drink it down. As they passed the Albert Bridge, the starlings were flickering in formation above and, on the streets, bright-eyed people were merging on the city, infused by party fever. The soft pink of the sky made everyone glow like they had caught the sun that day.

Luke Kelly was waiting just by the doors of the Park Inn Hotel. She was surprised to see he was no more than about nineteen. He was looking out nervously from under the eaves. There were no kisses for her or even a handshake, just a curt hello. She followed him up to his room, understanding he was frightened of being seen with her.

After a quick fumble with his keycard they were in the room.

'Sorry, but I didn't want my teacher to catch me,' he explained in an American accent. 'But it's all cool now,' he grinned.

He was from New York and was studying at a Bible college in England, but he was part of group of students spending a month in Ireland. He was soft-spoken and shy. His hair was shaved short emphasizing his fine features.

'Where's the rest of your group? Don't tell me, drinking Guinness in the pub.'

'No,' he laughed. 'They're with girls too.'

He'd had quite a few girls, he said. He took off his jacket which looked two sizes too big for him, like he was a kid playing at being a man.

He was slender under it. She slid out of her dress, watching his eyes on her. Under his sweatshirt, he was wearing a long white t-shirt. The sight of him reminded her of a virgin girl in a shift on her wedding night.

On the bed, he kissed one of her thighs gently, then the other. She noticed his skin was as soft as hers. Aroused, he licked his fingers to make them wet and touched her, as if anointing her. When she sucked him, he sighed. Just before he climaxed, his chest and neck reddened with the blood-rise and she could feel the passion in him.

Afterwards, as they lay in bed stroking one other, he told her he was engaged to a girl back home. They'd had dates but because of their religion he wasn't going to sleep with her before marriage. Back in America, he said, he even went out to bars to drink, but now he was studying, he couldn't.

'Better go now and meet my teacher,' he said, making a face. 'The guy watches us like a hawk.'

'No problem,' she said. She got dressed quickly and he saw her to the door.

'Listen, Mia, would you be able to see me outside the agency?' he asked. 'I could pay you direct.'

'Yeah,' she said, without really thinking, as she liked him. She gave him her number.

A quick, chaste kiss and she left.

She waited for a taxi outside. Moths flitted about like bits of scattered parchment from old torn scrolls. She wondered if she'd done the right thing in giving him her number. The taxi driver wanted to chat, but the sex had lulled her into quietness. For her, sex always felt like the exorcism of wild spirits within. Some people went on crazed drunken benders, some filled themselves with drugs, others worked so their bodies ached, but sex was the one thing that had always sated the energy in her.

The taxi passed some homeless people lying wrapped in duvets in the doorway of Linen Warehouse. Behind them, the bright shop windows showcased beds covered in sparkling fresh white linen. The driver headed on towards the darker streets of the East. As he stopped at the traffic lights, two boys were shadow-fighting under the footlights that illuminated Willowfield Church. Their shadows were huge, stretching up the brickwork, nearly touching the tip of the spire. They stopped fighting to look up in almost spiritual wonder at their own images stretching far beyond them.

She met Sean for a drink the following week at the John Hewitt.

'A pint of Carlsberg,' she said to the barman.

'Jesus, very sophisticated, aren't you?' mocked Sean.

'Don't worry,' she laughed. 'I ordered wine with Mr Woolf.'

Sean asked for an Irish Ale. There was a chalk board above the bar listing the differing complexions of ale: blond, red, pale, white, like they were women.

'So, how was Luke Kelly?'

'Shy, sweet. Not the most conventional of biblical scholars!'

'He's probably doing forty days of penance right now,' Sean laughed. 'But at least you released the pressure there, Mia. You probably purified him.'

He started telling her about the ethos behind starting the agency with Marcus, his Jamaican partner. He wanted the agency to be European in concept, for the purposes of healing minds, of providing spiritual comfort to the lonely rather than some sort of crude, quick sex purveyance.

She was surprised by his lofty ideals. 'I hadn't thought of you as some sort of hippy,' she grinned.

He told her about the time he'd visited a brothel in London and how the woman had been rough and impatient with him. 'Sex is about kindness and generosity,' he posited. 'I don't want a cold business.'

'But what if people take advantage of you?' She thought of Luke. He'd phoned her the previous night but she'd missed his call. 'What if one of the girls takes the numbers of your customers and starts a rival firm?'

'If they did, they'd be in trouble. If Marcus found out...' trailed off Sean darkly. 'He's beaten Lucy in the past, you know.'

'Oh, God.' She immediately understood why Marcus stayed behind the scenes and let Sean be the suave frontman. Good cop, bad cop. 'But Lucy's so nice.'

'Yes, and the clients love her too.'

'Marcus makes her work?' she asked, outraged.

'No. She wants to. She's open.' He smiled at her quizzically. 'God, you're not very modern, are you?'

After a couple of drinks, he invited her back to his flat. He had wine there, he said, and she thought to herself, why not. She was having fun with him.

He lived in an apartment near the Waterfront. The kitchen was white and new, but sparse in a way that revealed its occupier was rarely there. He explained that he'd moved in after a recent divorce. He vaguely cited his ex-wife's difficulties with his 'progressive ideas'. Rachel imagined him saying, 'You're not very modern,' to his wife when she'd complained about his other women.

The living room surprised her. In its centre was a sofa covered in multi-coloured drapes. Paintings and posters crowded the walls. The air was full of the smell of candles and incense. As usual, when she saw bookcases wedged with books, she made a beeline for them. Sean's taste in literature, she noted, was similar to hers — *On the Road*, *The Doors of Perception*, *Lolita*, *Nausea* — the books written by life's outsiders.

He lit some candles and poured the wine. Rachel sat down. She shifted some forms on the coffee table to make room for her glass. She noticed the name on them was Dermot Heenan.

'Hey, Dermot.'

'Yep, my real name's Dermot and I'm from Armagh. Very exotic,' he commented wryly. 'You think I'm going to run an escort agency under my own name? Anyway, we're all about illusion here, aren't we? Tonight, you are Mia and I'm Sean.'

They clinked glasses. He picked up a book on Timothy Leary, and tossed it to her.

'You know him?'

'Sure. LSD guru.'

He rummaged around in a drawer and, when he came back over, he opened his palm to her.

'Ever tried it?'

He held out two tabs of bright lemon blotting paper.

'I have now,' she said, popping one into her mouth. She'd once had some mushroom tea at university that had given her no more than a light buzz.

They discussed the different drugs they'd taken and Sean talked with hierophantic fervour of how he was experimenting like Timothy Leary with higher doses. The acid slowly started taking hold of her. The candlelight grew brighter and cast large soulful shadows on the wall.

'Look, look at the boats!' exclaimed Sean, pointing out the Paul Klee poster. A flotilla of sailing boats were dipping their flickering oars into the sea and seemed to be powering to the shore. Next to it, a red poster was embering gently like a warm fire.

Sean leant over and kissed her. His blue eyes were spinning, his blond hair sparked.

'Oh, God, I shouldn't,' he said, drawing back. 'Marcus told me not to mess with the girls.'

The room got darker a second; snakes in the shape of dread-locks hissed in the corner.

'Keep hold of the light, Sean,' she said, kissing him back.

She couldn't stop kissing him. He was mesmerizing. She'd found him charismatic from the first time she'd met him.

They began to touch, to paw at each other in longing. Within time, their clothes seemed to melt from them. Their bodies were almost impalpable. While Sean leant over her on the sofa, Klee's oars kept driving into the waves behind his head.

One of the candles burnt down and the room got darker once more. Little dark cartoon characters edged into her eyeline. There was something in the acid that came out in the black.

'Light another candle, Sean,' she urged.

The new light arced through the room with a hummingbird quiver.

She woke up beside Sean in his bed. A stream of sunlight was angling in on her from the barely closed curtain. She checked her watch. The hands on it seemed jittery but she just about made out that it was ten a.m. Her eye was drawn to a fold in the duvet that resembled the curving concaves of a naked woman lying on her side. She realised it was still the acid playing tricks.

She wanted to sleep some more, but she was wide awake now, jammed between the cold wall and the heat of Sean. She looked across at him. His eyelids seemed to be tremoring under deep, seismic dreams. He looked so vulnerable she felt a yearning for him. She remembered his high-minded visions for the agency and leant over, kissing him on the shoulder. She slipped out of bed, and Sean turned but didn't waken.

Later that afternoon, her mobile rang. At first, she was glad to see it was Sean as she couldn't have faced anyone else. She'd tried to go back to bed, but there were still traces of the drug in her system.

The last thing she was expecting was for Sean to tell her that she had a client that night. The client wanted her for the whole night too. He lived out in Broughshane, but not to worry, as Sean would take her there.

Even as Sean was speaking, she saw in the curtains another reclining woman with large hips and breasts like a Renaissance figure. The image kept haunting her.

'I can't, Sean,' she said, in horror. 'I feel totally strung out.'

'But you have to. None of the other girls are free.'

He was angry with her, insistent. She understood that, in spite of the night they'd spent together, he still saw her as an employee.

'But it was your fault,' she pointed out, 'for giving me that tab.'

'But what am I going to tell Marcus?'

She was firm about being in no fit state and Sean huffily agreed to postpone the client for another week and rang off.

She paced around, thinking things were getting out of control. She hated the idea of being called at the last minute for sex-on-demand. She was tired, agitated. She hadn't properly considered that an escort always had to be on call. It was a lifestyle, not a job.

She turned, hearing Stephen breeze in from work.

'Hey, how's you?' Stephen asked.

'Good, good,' she said, retreating from him into the kitchen.

'Any more dates?' he called after her, teasing.

She thought feverishly of ways out. Making a quick decision, she rang a number.

'Hello, Delta Properties,' sang the composed English accent.

English accents always made her feel provincial and inferior but she tried to inject confidence into her voice. 'Yes, may I please speak to John Woolf?'

'He's away on business but I could take a message. What's the name of your company please?'

'Ah...it's no company,' she stumbled, hearing the apology in her own voice. 'It's just me. Tell him it's Mia Lewis.'

'No problem,' said the girl. Rachel imagined her saying to the rest of the office with a smirk, 'Yet another one of John's women.'

After she'd rung off, she wondered if she'd been speaking to his ex-escort girlfriend. Even if he did get her message, she was sure now he wouldn't phone back. The more she thought about it, the more it had just seemed like John's gamble on the night, a dare just to add frisson to the whole encounter, another game for him to play like the blackjack. And now that she'd dared him back, it was too late and he was already on to the next fantasy.

She wasn't sure if she could even leave the agency if she asked. She thought about the photos of her in her underwear she'd sent to Sean. She'd got a girlfriend to take them under the pretence they were for a new boyfriend. She hated that Sean and Marcus had something to blackmail her with. God, the paranoia was kicking in. She had to stop it now.

She lifted a beer from the fridge and cracked it open. In the ring pull, she saw again the faint contours of a reclining woman. Changing her mind, she chucked the contents down the sink and ran the tap till it was icy. She filled a big glass and drained it.

Another call came through on her mobile. It was her mother. Rachel hadn't called her in a while and instantly felt guilty.

'I'll be over next week, Mum,' she heard herself say, knowing she couldn't face her parents any time soon. It was at least easier to lie on the phone than in person. She'd already told them she'd got another job in an office only this time it was better paid. 'Work's very busy right now.'

'Dad says he's impressed you haven't asked us for money all month,' said her Mum.

'Yeah. I thought I'd give his wallet a wee break,' Rachel said lightly.

'I know it's been difficult for you with the economy the way it is. Your cousin's still looking for work, so it's brilliant you found something.'

She could hear the swell of pride in her mother's voice at her new independence. It made her ache inside. Surely she couldn't give up the agency yet, not until she'd proved to her parents she could stand on her own two feet.

'We're so happy you're doing well now, Rachel. We love you so much.'

The next week, Sean called her. He didn't refer to her letting him down, but simply asked if she was free to see the Broughshane client.

He told her all about him. Peter Maxwell was an antiques dealer, in his fifties, and was something 'high up in the Orange Order'.

'What is he, King Billy's grandson?' joked Rachel.

'I think he needs a bit of a release from his repressive life,' Sean said, taking it seriously.

'Don't worry, I'll be good to him,' she assured him.

The following night, Sean picked her up. He was driving her to Broughshane, dropping her off at Peter Maxwell's house, then returning to Belfast. Peter had requested an all-nighter for four hundred pounds and she was somewhat edgy about being stranded out in the country with him. Hotels always felt safer.

At the bottom of her street, some kids were lying on the ground, playing dead, chalk-marking each other.

'I know how they feel,' she said.

'Come on. The Grand-Master-of-the-Lodge, or whatever he is, is probably very nice. I'll be checking him out too, remember, and if I get a whiff of weirdness off him, I'll whip you out of there so fast...'

They headed north, chatting lightly. Ruffled clouds, golden-tinged, peeked over the tops of the mountains. She enjoyed the zip of the passing countryside and the smoky, burnt tang of wood fires. There was a cold nip in the air. She'd already paid off her debts, but with more fees like tonight's maybe she could think of a trip somewhere. Money was freedom. She'd just have to be colder about this job, grow some ice round her heart. She thought of the impending winter and of the frost flowering on the ground and how it made things more beautiful.

It was getting dark by the time they turned into Peter Maxwell's drive. It was a large sandstone house on the edge of Broughshane, secluded from the road by firs. Twin lanterns were shining by the front door but there was no light from the windows. Her first thought was of Bates Motel.

Sean had no such qualms. 'Very impressive,' he marvelled, as he rolled the car to a stop. 'Know what? We should have asked for five hundred.'

Peter Maxwell was already at the front door.

'I'm Sean Hilton and this is Mia Lewis,' said Sean cheerily, shaking his hand.

When Rachel shook Peter's hand, it felt dry and hard.

They went through to the living room. The house was full of busy carpets, she noticed, and clutter. Sean, on the other hand, was fascinated by the clutter which apparently was comprised of very expensive antiques.

Peter poured them both some wine. She noticed he was slim and still had plenty of black in his hair, but he looked careworn.

'This is a beautiful piece,' burbled Sean about a vase, doing his best to be a one-man party atmosphere.

'Yes, she certainly is,' Peter said, putting a hand on Rachel's leg as he sat down beside her. Peter cackled at his own joke. Rachel managed a half-hearted smile and shot a look at Sean.

Peter talked about his business a while. Sean sat there uncomfortably, making the right responses. She could feel his worried eyes on her. She wished he'd pull her out of that cold house. The room felt fusty. She'd always disliked antiques as they belonged to the past and she only really cared for the present.

'Right, I'm off,' Sean announced, jumping up. 'The long drive back and all.'

He kissed Rachel goodbye, clasping her tight to show Peter how much she meant to him.

'Bye,' she said, feeling abandoned. But it was business and she knew she'd no right to expect love or sympathy.

She followed Peter upstairs. There were about six or seven doors leading off the landing.

'My housekeeper's left us everything we could want,' he told her happily.

He opened the door into his bedroom. A peat fire was blazing and the lamps were bright. He took the champagne out of its ice bucket and popped it with a lone cheer. A tray of roast chicken and strawberries lay on a table.

'See? We don't have to leave the room all night,' he smiled, clinking glasses with her.

He kissed her and began to undress her. His fingers were thin, nimble and had the texture of crepe. He pinched her bra open without her even feeling it and she guessed he was so used to handling fine things, he knew the art to it. They held each other, but his penis was flaccid. She did everything she could to breathe life into it.

'Give it a bit more time,' he urged, falling back into the pillow as if from a great height. 'It's been so long for me.'

His wife had been twenty years younger, he explained. She'd left him a year ago and he hadn't had a woman since. He'd only found out about her cheating after he'd had a trip to the clinic and been told he had a sexual infection. Finally, she admitted she'd been with a lot of different men and he threw her out.

'God, what a dark tale,' shivered Rachel.

They tried to make love again. Every time he showed a glimpse of tumescence, she tried to slip a condom on, but it kept sliding off.

'Don't bother about the condom,' he sighed.

'But I have to,' she insisted.

At about the fifth go, she gave up. She let him inside her. She felt the low beating within her, as at last the blood rushed into him.

Afterwards, he rolled back from her.

'If you give me a disease, I'll track you down and kill you,' he warned, his breath still rasping. 'Don't think that I won't.'

The perversity of the threat chilled her to the bone, but she was almost too tired from the strain of pleasing him and the heat of the stifling room to care. He turned out the lamps and all they had was the glow of the fire. She wanted to sleep but he kept waking her up all through the night, like a man intent on drinking his fill after a long drought. She could hear a stir in the chimney and, at about five a.m., a threnody of winds was thrumming softly in its flue.

'You're so beautiful,' he kept murmuring.

He was the first up in the morning and threw back the curtains on the stage setting of the hills of Broughshane.

'You don't have to go straight home, you know,' he said wistfully. 'We could walk into the village, have breakfast and then you could come back with me.'

'No, I have to be back early. I've so much to do,' she said, springing out of bed, dying to escape, but anxious not to offend him. Even in daylight something about him scared her. 'Can you please drive me to the train station?'

She quickly got dressed. His wardrobe door was open and she caught a glimpse of the orange of his sash within. It looked worn and faded.

On the train home, she looked out at the dolorous, lavender skies above. The countryside had a raggedy autumn feel to it. A couple of slits of light appeared through the slatted sky, then disappeared. On the run down into Belfast, a haze bleached the cityscape below into a pale grey that matched the lough. When the rickety train finally pulled into Central Station, the Belfast hills were bomb-black.

Her mobile rang.

'So, how was the Grand-Master-of-the-Lodge himself?' went

Sean's cheery voice.

She couldn't say anything. She just wanted to cry.

'What? What did he do to you?' he demanded tensely.

'Nothing. It was just a nightmare.' She told him about not being able to use a condom and the dark talk of diseases. 'I can't do this any more, Sean.'

'Come on, you're just tired. You're a really strong girl.'

'I'm not.'

It was over. This play-acting at something she wasn't. She wasn't emotionally detached enough. She didn't have that ice in her bones and she had too much white heat in her imagination. Sean wanted her to think over her decision, but she'd made up her mind. The one thing she needed was the photos and she asked him if he'd go to the office and remove her page from their files.

'I'll try but Lucy keeps a pretty sharp eye on it,' he promised uncertainly. 'You know, I felt terrible to leave you there yesterday. All the way home I thought about you.'

Late the next afternoon, she met Lucy at Central Station. Lucy handed her the white envelope with three hundred pounds in it while all the commuters passed by in a blur. Rachel chatted lightly and didn't mention anything to Lucy about leaving the agency. She was scared that Marcus would kick up rough. It was best that Sean deleted her file as if she'd never existed. Mia was dead.

'One question,' said Lucy just before she left. 'Marcus wants to know, has Sean ever tried it on with you?'

'No,' said Rachel. 'Not at all.' It didn't even matter to her if he'd been with every girl in the agency. Whatever he'd done, she wasn't going to betray him.

As she walked back to East Belfast, the blue sky was faintly ridged with white cloud, making her dream of crested waves. She thought of all the options in her life. She could always go back to university to study teaching. She breathed freely. The autumn trees were starting to cast off their leaves and quivered in the breeze as in a shy striptease.

She'd only been in the house five minutes before there was a knock on the door. The knock became more and more urgent and she ran to it, panicking. It was Sean. He was in a bad way. His suit was disheveled and he looked utterly shell-shocked.

'Sean, are you okay?'

He turned his cheek to reveal a giant indigo bruise.

'Christ! What happened?'

'Marcus.' Sean was shaking as he walked through. He'd come straight from the office. He'd been sitting deleting Rachel's file when Marcus had come in on him.

'He said that I'm too soft with the girls. He's gone fucking mad. He thinks you're all stealing our clients from us.'

'Oh, no.'

'See? He punched me! I thought he was going to kill me. Now he's locked me out of the office for good. He said you couldn't leave, he'd never let you leave but, look, I got you the hardcopy.' He produced the photo she'd sent him.

She tried to take it from him, but he held it tight. 'Can I not keep it?' he asked. 'I love this photo.'

'No, I have to have it,' she said, not trusting him.

'Oh God,' he breathed out. It was if his eyes were writhing. 'Make the snakes go away. It's like I'm being punished for loving you too much.'

'How many tabs did you take?' she asked.

'Two. Please hold me.'

She held him. She was thinking of all his exhortations to be kind to the clients.

'Oh, Mia,' he sighed.

'I'll get you a drink,' she said, going into the kitchen, needing one herself. For all she knew, Marcus still had her details and it terrified her.

She could hear her mobile going off in the living room.

She ran through to get it, but Sean was already looking at the name of the caller.

'Luke Kelly,' he said, stunned. 'You stole him. *You*…you fucking went against us.'

'I didn't mean to, he persuaded me,' Mia muttered, shrinking from his cold, blue stare.

'You've done a stupid, stupid thing. Marcus will go mad when he finds out.'

'Please, Sean.' She stepped closer to him, hearing the tension in her own voice. 'You don't have to tell him.'

'True, I don't have to but I should. Maybe I won't. But you can't just dance away from all this.' He nodded to himself, deciding. 'This is what I'm thinking. We'll keep it to ourselves for now. You be good to me, Mia, I'll be good to you…'

He pulled her tight against him. She could feel his hand moving up to the back of her head, as her body locked into his grip.

WHAT SHE DOES IN THE DARK

It was a blister of an afternoon in early August when Fiona saw her son's living ghost in the graveyard. It was one year since Jack had died and the earth was well-settled now above him with not so much as a wraith of a breeze. It was too hot even for the birds and it seemed like the whole world was on a minute's silence. A bee buzzed by, breaking the spell. But how different it was from the rainy day last August when the rusty orange earth was opened raw, the nameless number on the bare plot like a prisoner's number, like the tomb of the unknown soldier killed in action, killed by *in*action… She shivered, but everything was okay now, she was less strung-out, she was getting over it.

A strand of clover was sprouting from the grass and she knelt to remove it, but stopped herself. Jack had been wild in life, so let it flower. She got to her feet, ready to impart some last expiatory words to Jack, but she couldn't shake off the ridiculous thought that she'd dressed him up too formally in his coffin and he'd still be angry with her. Looking up, she noticed two figures coming down the hill towards Jack's plot. One was her ex-partner, Alex, with…she caught her breath. The boy had hair blond and messy as hay, the same strong chin. It was Jack's cousin, Warren. She hadn't seen him for years, not since Alex's brother had moved to Belfast for work. As she walked towards them, she said hello. Only Warren bothered to answer.

She drove back into the city over the Peace Bridge. There was some new urban poetry on one of the walls:

Get high and you'll die,
Take heed, no speed,
This is your last warning.

The Dissidents were behind it. Dissies against the druggies. It was a brutal but effective message. The Catholic Bogside had always controlled drugs better than the small Protestant enclave of the Fountain. Since Jack had died, she'd been trying to get more anti-drug initiatives off the ground but the Fountainers weren't keen on admitting they had a problem.

She turned under the arch into the Fountain. The first six houses on each side of the road were derelict, but the boarded windows had curtains painted on them, vases, even a sleeping cat on the windowsill to take off the rough look. The lamp posts were decked out in pristine flags of Red Hand and Derry Crimson. She headed on past the bonfire that rose up like a huge honeycomb in front of her. Londonderry's walls loomed behind, the stones baking in the heat, black as the crust on molten lava, and one touch would have seared the hand off you.

A coach pulled up ahead of her outside the Fountain Youth Club where she worked. The coach was full of young Scotsies, bandsmen from Ayr, coming over early for the big Apprentice Boys' parade. They streamed out, die-hard bravehearts sweating in their kilts, knees pink as bacon, voices fluting in the air. She jumped out to greet them and, all around her, a crew of Fountainers were rushing up, offering their floors to the incomers. It was like a scene from a livestock market, the mostly female Fountainers choosing which of the young, fit Scotsies caught their eye.

'Here, I'll squeeze you in,' said a woman, pinching one of the guy's biceps. 'Any room at the inn with you, Fiona?'

'No chance.' There was no way she was opening up her house to anyone. She hadn't slept for nights, running her mind over Jack, and the exhaustion in her ran as deep as the battlements.

That evening, the welcome party was in full swing at the Memorial Hall. The bar was four-deep and a Scots accordion band was playing on stage. From Ayr, Fiona thought to herself, wishing she was from a place that sounded so light. It wasn't easy coming from Londonderry, the most contested city in Europe — on every country road the sign for Londonderry had the London sprayed out.

She noticed Warren standing shyly on his own, while Alex chatted to his cronies. She still marvelled at how he was the spit of Jack. Even the way he was standing rubbing his eyebrow, unsure of himself. She went over to him.

'So, do you remember me?'

'Course I do. You took us to the beach last time.'

'That's right, you and Jack. You must have been eight,' she said and for the first time she noticed she was able to say Jack's name out loud without a stab of pain.

They'd hardly begun chatting when Warren was pulled away by a tide of teens. She guessed they were joshing him about hanging out with the oldies. Alex was looking over at her, but she glanced away. Seventeen years together had been obliterated in that one night exactly one year ago.

That night, Jack had been out guarding the bonfire with his friends. They'd all been taking ecstasy. He'd been standing on the top of bonfire when he'd fallen. One of his friends said that it looked as though he had stepped off...

Have a brain-bleach, he's off his bollix, steamboats, off on the whirlybirlies, lit to the tits, there's no brakes on a rocket, she's licking the windies, you daze-ball, skull it, lash it into you...

She woke up with a start. All these voices — she didn't know if they were in her head or her ears. Colliding echoes of the past. She got up and stumbled to the window. The words belonged to the teenagers sitting round the bonfire, their voices rising high on drink and drug-lifts and meph-meanderings. She thought about going out and giving off to them, but there was scant point as the bonfire had to be guarded every night before the burning.

It was 03:02 by her mobile. Christ. In about eight hours, she had a presentation to give to some councillors on her new anti-drugs initiative. She had a rummage in her drawer for sleeping pills. Next to them, she found a tiny bag of marijuana buds she thought she'd thrown out. She'd smoked them in the first weeks after Jack's death as a kind of communion with him, in the mad idea that she could find him in the smoke, even though it was really just to deaden her head from the self-beration. The night after the funeral, Alex had let rip, accusing her of being too involved with community work to care what was happening with their son. But, him, hadn't he been caught up in his petty drug-deals and of all people he should have seen the signs of drug abuse.

Enough, she told herself abruptly. What was the point of replaying it all?

She threw the bag in the bin and popped two pills, standing at the window till tiredness overtook her, till the tendrils of heart-coloured pink began creeping in from the east and the teenagers' tones lowered into the gentle chant of an incantation.

The next day was hotter still. The alcohol from the previous night fairly steamed off the skin in the glitterball of a sun. As she walked back from her presentation, she bumped into a couple of Alex's mates. Squat, steroided up, they both fired her hard looks. They didn't like her working with councillors from the Bogside.

Warren was lounging on the steps of the youth club with his t-shirt off. She took the suntan lotion from her bag and tossed it to him.

'Factor thirty!' he mocked. 'That's for babies.'

'Go on, use it,' she urged and stood over him, watching him butter it into his skin with the blades of his fingers. It was the same skin as Jack's. She tried not to look but couldn't help herself. There was even a tiny mole on his shoulder that was identical. He threw the lotion back to her and lay back down on the steps. The bottle was sticky from his hands and she went inside to run it under the cold tap.

That evening, the streets outside Fiona's house were hiving as everyone headed to the Memorial Hall. Fiona looked at herself in the mirror. Pretty good, she reckoned, for thirty-nine. Her hair, tied back into a tight bud, was as dark red as dulse and she pulled a few strands out to soften it around the brow. She put more make-up on than usual, impressed by the sparkle of it on her skin. The wind was getting up outside. She'd always observed that people acted wilder in the wind.

In the Memorial Hall, she made eye-contact with one of the Scots guys, Eddie. Eddie was tall, broad and self-effacingly dressed in a checked shirt. He bought her a drink and, although he didn't say much, he complimented her with his widened eyes. She hadn't been with a man since Alex. It was strange but even a brief flirt with a man had felt like infidelity, not to Alex, but to Jack's memory. When the DJ kicked off, she and Eddie danced, clumsily from the drink, clattering the hands off one another with their moves. Alex scowled at her at one point which made her smile all the more at Eddie.

Later, she spotted Alex slipping a small bag into a teenager's hand in exchange for cash. Alex could hide drugs up his sleeve better than a magician. But how could he keep on selling after what happened to Jack? Was he just trapped in his old ways, under the siege-shadow like everyone else in the Fountain? Oh, of course he justified his selling as controlling the drugs that came into the Fountain, monitoring who took what, keeping out the more dangerous legal highs. Jack had died, he'd claimed, from rogue drugs brought in from the Bogside.

Her gaze moved round to Warren and she noticed he looked brighter somehow, blissed-up. He was hugging Courtney, one of the local girls. Fiona wondered if he'd dropped a pill but, just then, the lights flashed on harshly for closing time and the bar staff began to hurry everyone out the doors.

'Can I walk you home?' Eddie asked.

'No,' said Fiona, watching his face fall. Relenting, she added, 'Not tonight.'

As soon as she said it she regretted it. She didn't mean her kindness to give him false hope.

Outside, the wind had become stronger and the moon shone down weirdly as if a giant alien spacecraft was hovering above. Alex was saying a drunken goodbye to all his mates with the exaggerated fondness of an émigré. Fiona could see Warren up ahead, staggering off down the road towards the bonfire, drawn in by the whoops and moon-shot cries.

'No, no, Warren,' she said, running up beside him. 'Time for home.'

'What's it to do with you?'

His eyes were huge, impossibly molten with movement.

'Have you taken something?' she demanded, pulling him round into the beam of the street light. She looked into his face and it seemed that Jack was staring back at her. It startled her.

'Let's walk it off. Come on with me.'

She took him round the perimeter of the Fountain, showing him the old gaol tower that shone eerily in the moon's light like a gothic folly. A Sinn Féin councillor had once told her there were a hundred words for field in Irish. No wonder they fought so bitterly over this tiny scrap of land.

'So what are you? Just a page in a history book?' Warren teased. He was studying history for A-level. *Modern* history, he specified. She hadn't guessed he was into books.

When they reached Alex's house, she said goodnight to him. The wind was playing plangent notes on the rickety railing, plucking it like a harp. For seconds, she lingered on his face, unable to break away. She was looking for Jack, in the same way she kept scouring old photos for comfort.

Confused, he moved in, tried to kiss her. She felt the hot of his breath on her mouth before she pulled away, the fear skewering through her that someone would see them.

She returned to her house, scolding herself, resolving to keep her distance from him for the rest of his stay. She was his aunt for Christ sake, well, ex-aunt. He was only seventeen! The whirligig washing line was dervishing like a demon in the garden next to hers.

Fire it, buck it into them, brick them, bang them, kick them in the cookie, you haven't the swingers, empty the fuckin' hoorbags...

She woke up in a panic, a vision that Warren was in danger sirening in her head. There were yells at the bonfire. She staggered to the window and looked down the road to where the teenagers were swooping on the rubble of an old wall like seagulls feeding on bread. They were firing bricks over the perimeter fence and she guessed the Bogside youth had launched some sort of incursion. The moon beat down on the riot, a lurid ecstasy pill, the white powder of sprinkled stars circling the sky. Alex and another community worker were already running over to the young-bloods to stop them. Relieved there was no need of her, she sank back into bed.

The next day was the eve of the parade and the youth club was closed. Fiona woke late to a downpour rocketing onto her roof with the force of a snare drum. She dragged herself into the shower which also beat down on her hungover head with the cleansing effect of rain on a dusty road. From the snatches of drum and flute slivering through the air, she could tell that the bands were already congregating.

She got dressed and hurried out. Just outside the gate, she had to step over a smashed bottle of red alco-pop. The glass glimmered like rose quartz.

Her aunt, Leanne, was gardening a few doors down.

'You've caught the sun,' Leanne called out, grinning. 'Either that or you've done something to make yourself blush.'

Fiona dashed on, scared that someone had witnessed Warren's attempted kiss and spread it round the Fountain. On reflection, she realised Leanne was only teasing her about Eddie.

The rain had disappeared as quickly as it had come and the sun was splitting the trees. 'The sun always shines on the Protestant people,' boasted an elderly bandsman. The kids were waving plastic Union Jacks and licking red-white-and-blue candy canes. Warren was at the head of one of the bands, throwing his baton high in the air and catching it behind his back. Fiona couldn't keep her eyes off his muscles leaping like salmon in his arms and neck.

Alex sidled up to her.

'Fiona, we need to have a chat about all this anti-drug business.'

She was surprised. They had barely exchanged a word since the night of Jack's funeral.

'Yes. Okay, Alex.'

'I'll speak to you in a couple of days then,' he said in a friendly manner, before heading away. She imagined that having Warren with him was softening, healing him. She felt a pang that Alex was the one person who could ever share what she'd gone through. However, the thought of getting back with him alarmed her. Not talking was safer in a way.

She switched her attention back to Warren. He was twirling the baton and smiling at her. She smiled back, thrilled he'd noticed her above the young girls calling out to him. The next band up was Eddie's and he also shot her a big grin as he gave it 'the oul swagger'. It felt strange to have men looking at her. It was as if she had thrown off her mourning pall overnight and turned into flesh.

As Fiona walked home, the sun was shining through the stained glass windows of St Columb's, turning them into strips of throbbing disco lights. Some of the teenagers ran up the pallets to the top of the bonfire and affixed a tricorn hat to the effigy of Lundy. Overseen by Alex, they hung a placard saying 'Lundy the Traitor' round its neck. One of the kids shouted out joyously to Fiona, 'See? Our bonefire's so big you won't need your heating on for a month!'

At about seven, the DJ started up outside, belting out summer club anthems like they were all at an Ibiza beach party. Fiona couldn't stop thinking about Warren. He was quite different from Jack, now she thought about it. His hair was more honey-blond, his face was more defined; or was that just because her image of Jack was shrinking next to this real, living boy.

The words came back to her from the minister's commendation:

Jack has died in Christ's peace. He has come back to our Heavenly Father's house.

How inappropriate the whole service had been. There had been no peace in Jack, just as there was none in Warren either. That wildness in Warren was what kept drawing her to him. She checked her watch. It was nine. She looked out and saw the departing sun blow a last few kisses of pink cloud up to the sky and decided to go out.

The bonfire was thronging with people. Some of the teenagers were already weaving about like pollen-drunk bees. Her eyes quickly rooted out Warren. He was standing with his arm round Courtney. She was honestly relieved to see it, truly glad he had chosen someone to be with that night. Alex, she noticed, was in the shadows, doing his usual dealings.

Eddie came over to her and they clinked beers. It crossed her mind that tonight she should give him her body. She thirsted for closeness, wondered if it would release her.

As the sky darkened, the glo-tubes that the kids were wearing gleamed in bright acids. The DJ stopped his set just before midnight and a Scottish pipe band struck up ceremonially for the teenagers who trooped down with their torches to light the bonfire. To Fiona's surprise, Alex had arranged for Warren to be one of the lighters. She watched Warren run up the fiery side of the bonfire, bits of wood buckling under his feet. At the top, he set fire to the wood around the Lundy. He stood up there, arms outstretched, twirling the torch like it was a baton.

Jack, Jack, Jack, went a scream in her head.

'Get down to fuck, Warren!' Alex yelled behind her.

Warren ignored him, revelling in the adulation of the crowd while Alex barged through the onlookers, still shouting. Warren waited till the flames roared higher, then finally leapt through them onto the grass to cheers. He shrugged to imply it was no big deal. Alex barrelled over and gave him a mock-punch but in no time was playing it cool himself, laughing about it with his mates.

The heat began to drive everyone back. The DJ sparked up the decks once more and the party went into mad-melt-mode. With the amp-up, the teenagers ramped up the fevered dancing, undergoing a metamorphosis — a *meph*amorphosis, thought Fiona. Eddie was staring hypnotized into the fire. Fiona looked at him, noticing how the heat was flushing his skin. She really liked Eddie but what was the point when he'd only be heading back to Ayr after the parade. She took her chance and sneaked away.

She walked round the Fountain, enjoying how the ravey beats behind her pierced the quietness of the night. Behind a low wall, she spied a young couple having sex and suddenly wondered from the bangles and white hoodie if it was Courtney.

'Hey!' she called out impulsively, half-dreading to see Warren.

Courtney turned, panting, revealing the red, sweating face of one of the Scotsies beneath.

Fiona lowered her head, embarrassed, and walked on. Behind her, the Scotsie pleaded in deep, tumescent moans for Courtney to keep going.

Fiona was almost at Bishop's Gate when she heard footsteps behind her. She turned.

It was Warren. They looked at each other, felt the same prickly heat, felt the world contract till it contained only them.

'Come on with me,' she said.

At her door, the key kept fumbling in the lock. They stumbled up the stairs in their haste, as if their passion was being sabotaged by the house. They plunged through her bedroom door onto her bed. The bed post knocked against her knee, telling her, screaming at her through pain not to sleep with a seventeen-year-old. Alex's nephew.

'No. Let's just lie here for a while,' she urged, calming him down. She stroked his face gently, in a sisterly way, then stroked his arms, but the way he kissed her neck, the heat of his breath, made her writhe and she let him open her blouse and her fingers began to claw at his clothes and in no time she was feasting on his young, hard body, still not able to feel it, like it was buried deep in some country coffin, far away from her, and it was him who slowed her down, breathing more deeply, sucking her into his rhythm and, finally, through hearing him, she could feel him and, in the last of the senses to return, she could see him. And she almost cried with happiness because she had created a new memory that could blot out what had come before... and finally she could rest and there were no youthful voices in her dreams...

Sssst, ssst, crack, ack, ack, ack, ppphhhhHHHH...

Her mind crawled out from under its rock of sleep. The light was orange and flickering behind her blinds. She clambered out of bed and drew them back.

A Lundy had been tied to the lamp post and set on fire. The placard was charred but the remnants of the word, traitor, still jumped out at her. Fear buzzed through her.

'What's up?' Warren asked sleepily.

'You have to go,' she said, throwing him his clothes. 'They know you're here.'

All she could think was that someone must have told Alex.

She opened the front door for Warren. The neighbours were already out in their dressing gowns, standing at their gates, mesmerized by the crackling effigy. As Warren scuttled away, they gazed at her with wondering eyes, but she quickly shrank back.

She closed the door, slumping against it for a second. She went back up to her room. She couldn't believe what she'd done — she was crazy! The wound she'd just inflicted on Alex. He effectively ran the Fountain, his influence could dictate who lived there and who left.

She opened the old Bible that had belonged to her grandmother and put her hand on it, praying. Decades ago, her grandmother had inscribed all the names of her children, even the name of the daughter, Christina, who had died at a few months old. A teardrop had smudged the ink as she'd written the name. It had given Fiona comfort that others in her family had felt such a loss. There was a quote by Van Gogh jotted down on the back page:

Normality is a paved road: it's comfortable to walk but no flowers grow.

She read the words aloud to herself again and again. She rubbed her fingers across her lips, recalling Warren's kiss.

Calmed, she looked out to the sclera of the sky, a dawn fog whitening it. The Lundy had finally burnt out. She went outside and pulled down the remains from the lamp post, its hot ashes anointing her head. Londonderry, Lundyderry, she kept thinking. Ayr. Ayr. Ayr.

Later, in the morning she got ready to go out, knowing she had to face the Fountainers. At eleven, she left the house. Leanne was in her garden watering her plants with a teapot, as her watering can had burst. Red poppies were glowing against her red brick wall. It was as though echoes of the Somme lived in these streets. Always the past lived here, you could never escape it.

'Don't go,' Leanne pleaded. 'Everyone knows.'

'I'll be fine,' said Fiona.

The bandsmen and locals were excitedly gathering by the Memorial Hall in readiness for the parade. She spotted Alex in his black suit and ceremonial sash, crisp, severe. The Fountainers fell quiet when they saw her. The hot liquid of fear sluiced up her throat.

'Paedo!' shouted out Courtney. 'Do you like wee boys, do you?' Fiona searched for Alex's eyes but he looked at her with such viciousness, she turned. She could feel the spear of everyone's gazes in her back as she hurried away.

She didn't feel safe till the front door clicked behind her. Surely she wouldn't have to leave. She was so close to signing the Fountain up to an anti-drugs scheme. It was to be the one last thing she could do for Jack, to make sure no one else there would die. She kept staring at the suitcase on top of her wardrobe.

A stone suddenly smashed against her window, spitting shards into her pillow. She ran over and looked out. She thought she could see Courtney's pale hoodie, the glint of silver, disappearing, but she couldn't be sure.

She heaved down the case and pulled out the drawers full of clothes, her fingers resting on the wood as she wondered what to take with her. A stillness came over her. She went back to the day of the funeral, the undertaker drumming his fingers impatiently on the coffin as it lay on the bier, while the minister mumbled his blessings. Alex, chalk-white, but bearing up beside her. And how the tears in folk kept welling up, followed by the laughter they all clung to like liferafts. And she saw herself touching Warren, not with the light touch of a resurrectionist, but with frenzy for life, not with the light breaths of an invocation, but with the rasps of an earthly desire that would keep on waking her, shaking her till the day she died.

THE WILLOWHERB DREAM

It was August in St James's and Michael could hear little clicks as the flies, drunk on the sun, kamikazied into the window pane. Outside, the street was wildly dappled with light. Some seeds floated past slowly on the air like the little, sleepy, dismantled parts of dreams. God, he needed to concentrate. He had one more image to choose for the exhibition and the deadline was only an hour away. He clicked through the batch he'd just downloaded... the old woman at Milltown Cemetery, great one, Bog Meadows at sunrise and, ah, Jordy and the boys, all cheekbones and cheekiness, looking 'cool as fuck' as they'd call it.

He caught a peripheral flash of white t-shirt from the street, the bouncy, up-on-the-toes swagger. It was Jordy himself. One of the IFA. They called themselves IFA (short for I'll Fuck Anything) in defiant mockery of the IRA. They'd stolen a few cars in St James's but recently some older men had taken them aside and read them the riot act. The boys often hung about at the end of Michael's street, drinking, toking and pilling, but Michael didn't mind. If anything, they helped patrol the street which at least meant his cameras were safe. They never even woke him up with their shouts and peals of laughter in the night. He'd always been a heavy, dreamless sleeper.

Michael saw that Jordy was sporting a swollen eye. He ran out, slinging his Leica round his neck.

'Hey, Jordy,' he called. 'What happened to the other guy?'

Jordy grinned and immediately winced with pain. His eye was mottled and tuberous, the stitches black as a crushed spider.

'It was him. Baseball-bats.'

He nodded towards a heavy-set man of about fifty who was getting out of his car up the road. Kevin Curran. Michael only knew the man to say hello to, but, as with a lot of people in West Belfast, Curran's reputation preceded him. He was a Sinn Féin councillor, the typical bad boy alchemized by the peace process into golden boy.

'He said I snapped his wing mirrors off but sure why would I touch an oul wreck like that? I'd only do a Merc or a Jag,' Jordy added with a wink that made Michael laugh.

Without thinking, Michael took a photo of Jordy.

'Can I have that after?' said Jordy. 'I've got to put in a claim.'

Michael said yes, but as soon as he spoke, he regretted it. He didn't want to get involved.

He turned to go back inside. From his door, six houses up, Kevin Curran was looking straight at him. Curran scratched his wrist, pushing back the cuff of his shirt sleeve to reveal a dark tattoo. Michael quickly moved out of sight.

The phone was ringing. It was Sinead. She'd been at the conference in Mayo since Monday. His body suddenly ached for her as though for a medicine. 'You're not working too hard, are you?' she asked solicitously, hearing the longing in him and confusing it for tiredness.

He told her about Jordy's black eye, but could hear her voice on the line stretch out like a summer evening, disinterested. It had been six months since they'd moved to St James's because of cheap rent, but already she found the area too rough and was talking of moving again. She didn't like him hanging out with the boys and seemed to take his empathy for them as a reproach to her for shunning them. Yet, the thing was they were great for his art. He was seeing them through a new prism and his portraits were more powerful than any before. It was their sheer lust for life mixed with poverty of expectation he kept capturing, the butterfly fragility under their hard faces, that luminous humour lighting the eyes.

'Can't wait to see you,' he said and they bye-byed for what seemed like an age, neither wanting to be the first to hang up, as if frightened they'd never speak to each other again.

He looked out. The shadows from the trees were moving across the road like a million sundials.

He jumped out of his car and took a shot of the bonfire towering up like a tiered wedding cake, two small boys perched on top like a bride and groom. He took it swiftly before the boys could react and drove off, excited. Further along the road, he saw another bonfire made of pallets, so beautifully constructed it resembled a beehive, kids buzzing round it. It was the anniversary of internment and, although the likes of Kevin Curran had tried to stop the bonfires, tried to package up the past and consign it to the Sinn Féin museum, up they sprouted demotically every year like ragweed through cracks in the pavement.

For the past month, he'd had strange symptoms. His hands shook and he had an impression of quivering waves through his body. Since then, he'd been even more driven by a ceaseless search for the killer image, as if by immortalizing life, he could immortalize himself. He'd only started taking photos in his twenties during the peace process, but he wished to God he could have been around during the Troubles. Okay, so it sounded callous but a lot of Belfast artists had made their names on the twisted, bloody aftermaths of bombings, on ripped-open skulls, on blackened bodies with the clothes blown off them. Now all photographers could do was hang around the peace walls and pretend they were brilliantly portraying the legacy of the Troubles.

He arrived back in his own street in the evening. Pristine tricolours hung above front doors leading into scraggy, unkempt hallways. Everywhere windows were open, gulping in the hot air. There was a light breeze and a kind of Mexican wave ruffled the bunting across the street. The tricolour above Kevin Curran's door was tangled and knotted from the wind in an emblem of struggle.

Struck by the image, Michael walked up and took a photo.

Just below, Kevin Curran came into focus at the window, open-mouthed like a fish just swum up from some murky pond. There was confusion in his face.

Michael smiled and nodded at him, but Curran turned away. You had to be careful in Belfast. The city pulsed with paranoia. The older people still walked quickly, their bodies close to the walls, as if whispering secrets to the bricks. Michael no longer went to riots, as the crowd would think you were in cahoots with the police and would turn on you, trying to grab your camera.

'Isn't it a lovely day?' his neighbour, Moira, called out. She was a small bleached blonde, neither rich nor vain enough to worry about her roots. 'Hot with a breeze. I hope hell is like this.'

They both laughed.

Jordy's crew were standing at the end of the street in their bright, fiery t-shirts, as tall as the willowherb growing up from the mossy walls.

He looked up at the sky. Bone white cloud stretched out in the blue like knots of vertebrae spreading out to ribs. Somehow, it was comforting. A scan of an angel, he thought to himself. Like God had died and his ethereal bones had been laid out above. Uplifted, Michael went inside.

Michael woke up hotly in the night. It was his first nightmare in years.

He dreamt he was searching for himself, going from room to room, when finally he found himself sleeping in a bed. He tried to shake his own body awake, then realised with horror that his flesh below was lifeless. He was nothing but a spirit but what could he do without a body? 'What am I going to do now?' he shouted out.

He was still sweating and shaking. His pillow felt like a wet cloud. It felt like he had gone ten rounds with his duvet. He got up. He was starting to feel more tired these days. It seemed as though the body was trying to pull down the brain. It could be a number of things, the consultant had said, pursing her lips. He was waiting for the test results to come back. He knew something was wrong though and was scared that the parameters of his life would shrink, in the same way a lens kept narrowing its focus, smaller and smaller.

He could hear one of the boys whooping at the end of the street. It was only a silly dream, he said to himself. He was glad that Sinead was still away. Of course, she would have soothed him but it was better she didn't see him in a panic like this. He distracted himself by thinking about the exhibition and finally drifted back into a dreamless sleep.

Heat and light were flooding through his blinds, signalling yet another beautiful day. He got up, padded over to the window and opened the blinds. Shit! It was a shock. His car had been sprayed with silver letters.

He pulled on his clothes and ran out. 'IFA' was emblazoned down both sides of the car. Whoever had done it wasn't used to a spray can as the corner of each letter dribbled untidily.

'Fuck!' he said out loud.

Kevin Curran walked over from his house, a big, barrelling walk to show that he was the man to sort out any problem.

'It's those troublemakers again,' he said, nodding towards the end of the road.

'I suppose.'

'There's no suppose about it. Look, they've sprayed like a dog in the street.'

'I'll phone the police.'

Kevin Curran made a face.

'Are you mad? What'll they do? No, it's time we did something ourselves about these wee skiprats, yes?'

Kevin Curran affixed his gaze aggressively on him. He was a man who breathed hard as if to affirm his own presence.

'Well, I'm all about innocent till proven guilty,' Michael said.

'How are they innocent? Look what they've done with their own paw, eh?'

Michael nodded uncomfortably.

'Good. All these lot understand is affirmative action. We have to put the community first,' he said, trotting out the Sinn Féin-speak. 'I'll talk to some people today and get back to you.'

Kevin Curran walked away, satisfied. He got in his car and drove away.

Michael scratched at the graffiti with his thumbnail, hearing the scuff of trainer behind him.

It was Jordy.

'IFA. It wasn't fucking us, Michael.'

Michael looked at him, reserving judgment.

'I swear it wasn't us,' Jordy said plaintively. 'It was the IRA, that's who it was, it was him.'

He pointed at Kevin Curran's house.

'How would it be him?'

'He's trying to get us out. You don't know what he's like. Fuck me, they say when he was six he was the ammo man for the gunmen. He's psycho-city.'

'Look, Jordy. I know it wasn't you,' relented Michael.

'How could it be me anyway? I'd do a smart job, like. I'm like you, I'm a fucking artist.'

Michael couldn't help smiling. 'I know. I believe you.'

'No, you don't.' Jordy sloped away, muttering to himself.

Michael felt a pang of pity for the boy, mixed with frustration, and looked back at his car, annoyed. He'd have to drive to the garage, then take a taxi to the MAC. He'd overslept and had to be there by ten.

He had a last look up and down the pavement. There was a splash of silver shining like a star in the dark tarmac not far from the door of Kevin Curran's house. Surely it couldn't have been...

He went back into his house, wondering if it was all down to drugs. Jordy's crew bought their drugs from the Shankill and ignored the local dealers. But what was he doing, getting dragged into someone else's war? He was just relieved Sinead wasn't at home. Naturally she would have little sympathy, reckoning it served him right for siding with his 'little friends'. She couldn't see that this past month he'd needed their youth and wild spirit like a shot in the arm. He was only thirty-six.

He rushed into St Anne's Square. He saw the gym with its wall-to-wall windows, displaying clients running on treadmills. They looked like people in a hurry never getting anywhere, suspended for ever in glass. He went into the MAC and took the elevator up to the main gallery. Already, photos were being hung and some of them were stunning. He stared at the title: *Fifty Years of Belfast Exposed*.

The curator beamed at him. 'Your work, Michael, is just getting better and better.'

'Thanks,' he muttered without really looking at her. Everyone thought that he had a great future mapped out for him, but he wasn't so sure any more. All he knew he had for certain was the present. He poured himself a coffee and talked to her about a new solo exhibition.

It was late afternoon by the time he drove back, his car freshly resprayed. A little boy was leaning against Moira's wall, pulling at the juicy flesh of a leaf, stripping it to its skeleton. Michael took his photo. He was just getting his door key out when he spotted one of the boys flying down the street.

'Run, boy, run!' Michael shouted out cheerfully.

'It's Jordy!' the boy yelled in mid-flight. 'I'm getting help. Quick! He's in the entry.'

Michael shrugged, thinking it was probably nonsense but decided he'd better go and see.

He headed round to the alley. It was in shade, its walls glowing greenly with damp, a refuge from the heat. Its mouth was full of dark bins, but, further in, they'd all been knocked over as if in a fight.

He drew in his breath. Just behind one of the bins was a bloodied foot. The foil from a cigarette packet scudded towards it in the breeze.

He heard a moan, so low it might have been a creak from one of the ramshackle doors.

He threaded his way through the bins. Without thinking, he took a photo.

Jordy's face was slaked with blood. He'd managed to prop himself up on his elbows, but his jeaned leg lay twisted and broken, like an old roll of carpet thrown out.

'Jordy,' said Michael quietly.

Jordy opened his lips, his teeth pink with blood.

'I never…'

'I know,' said Michael. 'I know.'

The sound of a siren wailed. A boy from the IFA leapt over the bins and crouched beside Jordy.

'It's alright, mate, it's alright,' the boy crooned to him.

Michael backed away, alert to the siren, afraid of getting implicated. He stumbled out, his Leica cracking loudly against the wall, but he didn't care. All he wanted was to get out of that alley.

From his street, he could see the ambulance arrive, followed by a police car. He went indoors. A huge anger gripped him. He walked from room to room, not knowing what he was doing or why he went there. And it wasn't only Curran he was angry at, but himself. He had taken that photo in the alley knowing instinctively it would make him a winner. 'The Money Shot'. It was both news and art, the perfect combination. But where do you draw the line? Is that what he would want himself, photographers coming to the hospital taking records of him entitled *Portrait of a Dying Man*? He looked at his camera, thinking to yank out the film, to let the light destroy its grip over him, but he knew he never would, never could. He wanted that photograph. Because it was the truth. He sat down, put his head in his hands and cried.

After a while he went into the kitchen. He had to keep his strength up. He was starting to feel shivery, to not think straight. He threw together some pasta and tuna and added a sundried tomato sauce.

While he was eating, he could see a Romanian family who'd moved in nearby walking down the centre of the hot, dusty road, the boys with bedding slung over their shoulders, the mother pushing a pram with a mattress strapped to it. They strangely looked like a family evicted after a pogrom. Only they weren't; they were free to move where they liked. The city was changing, new people were coming and the beauty of it was that Curran didn't have a hold over them.

Two of Jordy's friends were sauntering along and Michael threw down his plate and ran out.

'What's the latest on Jordy?'

They told him he had a broken leg and multiple broken ribs, but he was stable in hospital.

'It was Curran who did it, right?'

'No way,' one of the boys said, looking at him like he was mad. 'He'd never bloody his own hands. It was his mates.'

'You didn't ask him to slap Jordy for fucking up your car, did you?' asked the other boy sharply.

'No, no, of course not,' said Michael, but he felt guilty. What was that Curran had said to him about speaking to some people? He should have said outright to leave Jordy alone.

He walked away, cowed.

Three more Romanian boys were coming down the street, sacks of potatoes draped over their slim teenage shoulders. Automatically, Michael raised his camera.

He felt a sudden tremor in his fingers and the image skidded out of focus. He pulled the camera back down. The Romanian boys were grinning and posing to try and get him to take more pictures. Hysteria grew in him. It kept happening. It was a feeling like the end of the world, this quake coming from within his own body.

He stepped back inside. He pulled the strap of the camera over his neck. He looked at his left hand, held it out horizontally. Not a tremor now. It was back to being solid.

There was a sharp rap on his door and he went to answer it.

It was Moira, his neighbour.

'I see your car's brand new again.'

'Yes, all fixed,' he said brightly.

She lowered her voice. 'Look, I know who it was. I've got it on camera.'

Michael felt a jolt. Of course. She had the security camera above her door, but he'd always assumed it didn't work it was so dilapidated. He'd paid no more attention to it than he had to the guttering.

'It was Curran?'

'Yes. And I want to put it on YouTube. Fuck him. To think people voted him in.'

She told him how her son had been bullied by Curran so badly he'd stayed in his room for two years. She'd only bought the camera in the first place as a warning to Curran.

'So, what do you say, Michael?'

She seemed happy to risk Curran's revenge, but Michael had to think, really think. He was ill now and didn't have the strength to fight. He had Sinead to consider. How could he drag her into all this?

His mobile rang, making him jump. It was almost as if Sinead knew when he was thinking of her. 'I'll only be a minute,' he said to Moira and walked back in.

'How are things?' Sinead asked.

'Great, good. Just out enjoying the sun.'

He'd already decided not to mention the car.

'All looking good for opening night?'

The care in her voice reminded him of the time they'd met for their third date. She'd been walking along the street, absorbed in her own world, her grey eyes steeled with thought when, seeing him approach, her eyes turned to the softest blue, like the Irish Sea being lit up by the sun. That was the moment he knew he'd stay with her.

'I can't wait to see you tomorrow,' he said.

'Are you definitely looking after yourself?' she checked, sounding worried.

'Sorry. I have to think about some press questions and it's all swirling around in my mind.'

'Yeah, I know you and your swirling mind, alright,' she laughed.

A few minutes later they said goodnight.

He went outside. Moira had gone in, but she'd left the door open into her hall.

He stood for a moment, feeling the sun on his arms. That was the thing about waiting around for a diagnosis. It was like the sun shone just for you every day. Everything looked different now, more intense, like moving to a foreign country. He looked at the leaves on the trees across the road, dancing on their stalks in the wind, full of life, while the few dead leaves scuffled about on the pavements, and he realised that he was alive, his heart suddenly began to leap as if on one of those stalks, and he knew that he had to make a difference in the world. The lens of his life might be shrinking, but every day he could feel its light getting brighter and brighter. Up to now his photographs at most had stirred the human soul of the viewer, but today, right now, there was an image that had consequence, sitting in Moira's house, something that could change things for the good, no matter what.

He rapped on Moira's open door. The wallpaper in the hall was white with pale blue flowers and it looked refreshing next to the yellow, scorching light. He walked over the threshold towards her. It was strange how strong he felt.

'Let's do it,' he said.

TWO PEOPLE SHORTEN THE ROAD

I look across at my passenger. He's sucking at the air as if his windpipe has shrunk to the size of a straw.

'Are you okay?' I ask.

'It'll pass,' he wheezes.

We're not far from his hotel. The satnav says it's the next left. I can still hear the unrest in his chest.

'Can you — take me to hospital?' he whispers haltingly.

'Are you sure?' I ask.

He coughs really hard, hacking through his fist, the air expelling through the narrow tube between his fingers. It's as if his lungs are trying to climb up out his chest into his throat and... when he pulls back his hand, his lips are almost white and there is red blood on his fingers.

For a second, I'm shocked, then I hit the brakes.

'Let's go,' I tell him, spinning the car round.

Fifteen minutes ago, it was a typical June morning. I'd pulled up in my taxi outside a nice house, big garden and I could smell the lilac in the fresh rain. I was thinking at least this job will be straightforward for, believe me, some of my customers are mad as mooncats, drinking so much they see triple not double! You should see it — after sundown all the vampires and werewolves coming out to play, and after sun-up foof! Gone like magic. Anyway, I was expecting the only trouble I'd run into today was the traffic.

After a while, the front door opened and a guy came out. He turned and kissed his wife who was crying and hugging him, but he was firm, insistent. Me, I was champing at the bit to get away. If taxi drivers got to start the meter before every goodbye, we'd all have fortunes by now.

My first guess was that he was going to work abroad but I sized up his suitcase as I opened the boot and it wasn't big enough for a really long trip. That's the thing about taxiing, you can't help guessing, pre-empting other people's stories. You keep meeting folk on the move, flying back from exotic locations. True, most have only been away in Ibiza and they're back looking like milk bottles after touring the inside of the nightclubs, but it still makes you think there's more to life. I keep having this nagging feeling that life is passing me by. Oh, don't get me wrong. Belfast has changed but if you're born here you tend to make like the Titanic and steam out of here at the first opportunity.

Anyway, the strange thing was I wasn't taking the guy to the airport. The depot said I was to take him straight to a hotel in south Belfast.

He finally got into the passenger seat and I was glad as I like having people beside me for the chat. Most folk go into the back like I'm their chauffeur, but there's an old saying in Irish: 'Two people shorten the road', meaning that a journey goes quicker when you're next to someone, having the craic.

This man, though, hardly spared me a glance. He was about forty, dark-haired with a few silver flecks, thin, nervy.

'That was a hard farewell,' I said to him.

'It was,' he grinned. His voice was too whispery for the look of him. His hands were crossed gently over his lap like two wings.

'South Belfast—that's not too far to go for a holiday,' I added wryly.

'It's no holiday,' he said. 'I'm going there to work for four weeks. To finish something I should have a long while ago.'

He had a lump of typed pages in a binder resting on his lap and the way he stroked it, it was like he was touching a holy relic, or even a lover.

'If I finish it,' he said, 'it'll help pay for my wife and kids.'

I wondered what it could be, but I decided to let him talk, uninterrupted. No matter how he kept justifying himself, I was sure whatever it was he was doing was for his own self-fulfilment.

'I love my family so much,' he was saying, 'but if I bring them along, I'll never get any work done. Oh, I know it's being selfish, but...'

'I can understand.'

'You can't but it's fine,' he shrugged, a corrosive cough scratching at his throat.

His hands were clasped. The thumbs were rolling around one another so tightly I suddenly thought of bodies thrashing around in the throes of sex. I found myself driving faster, spurred on by his need to get to the hotel.

'It'll be grand,' I told him.

'I hope so,' he said.

We stopped at the lights beside wild poppies growing along a brick wall. I glanced across at him, taking in his frail shoulders, and how there was a shudder through him now and then like a breeze. For some reason, I couldn't stop looking at him.

He was sitting there, dreamy-eyed, heavy-lidded with tiredness, but he was still so alert his eye swivelled to meet mine though his face didn't move an inch. It struck me what a secret observer he was.

'What?' he asked. 'Do I look sick?'

'Not at all. You look like a million dollars, pal. All green and wrinkly.'

We both laughed. For that's the taxi driver's job to brighten up your day with a bit of banter.

It wasn't long after that he started to cough up blood.

So here I am, racing to the hospital.

'We're not far now,' I reassure him.

He tries to speak but his lungs are erupting like a volcano. It's terrifying.

I speed down a side street, foot flat to the tin, even jump a kerb to skim round a car with its backend hanging out. I know the jolts are hurting him but he's wracked in half as it is. Up the Grosvenor Road I bomb and, hallelujah, I can see the statue of Queen Victoria at the Royal and I whisk into the ambulance docking bay.

The guy's head bobs back when I brake.

'Quick!' I shout out to a porter. 'He can't breathe.'

Two ambulance workers run out with a stretcher, apply an oxygen mask. I tell a nurse everything I know about the guy, read his name, address and phone number off the taxi smartphone. She touches my hand comfortingly, says he must have had a haemorrhage, promises they'll look after him. I'm that beside myself I almost forget to take his case out of the boot.

Diane from Dialacab is phoning me, wondering why I've gone AWOL, and I tell her what's happened. Straight away, she says to take a break.

I drive slowly into the city centre. It's lunchtime and I always pop into Barney's at this time for a fry or a burger. 'Barney's: Clogging Up Arteries since 1971' the sign boasts and, for once, I don't feel hungry at all. The rain has dried up and the sun starts to poke its head out the clouds like a toddler playing peekaboo. As I always tell the tourists, we don't have four seasons a year here, but we often have four seasons in a day. Across the road from Barney's I see a travel agent's with all these offers in the window — Istanbul, Bangkok,

Vegas... I suddenly shiver, thinking for the first time in my life it's not just the money that could hold me back, it's the time.

As I'm pulling away, I catch sight of the man's binder on the floor. What a prize dope I am — I should have left it in! I can't help opening it and reading the first page. Long words like 'transcendental' fly out at me, words that I have to think about, to find their meaning. Looks like fiction. A novel.

Later that afternoon, I phone the Royal but they can't give me any news other than the man hasn't regained consciousness. Maybe it isn't any of my business but I can't help thinking about him. It's not until the next day that I phone again and I'm put through to a ward sister who tells me that he died during the night, but that his family was with him.

All I can think is, I still have his book.

A week later, I phone Dialacab Diane and tell her I'm thinking of going to visit the writer's wife at her home. After all, I have the novel, and since I was the last person to speak to her husband it only seems right to deliver it in person. The words he said about loving his family — she has to know she was on his mind right to the end. But the truth is I'm thinking more about the need in myself. These past mornings I wake up to hear the pulse in my head like a second hand ticking. I need to know more about him, about everything in life. Every day I travel into Belfast, weaving through the city; part of it, but not truly in it. I'm only thirty and I want to really see the world for a change.

Taxi firms are usually dead against any fraternizing with customers but Dialacab Diane gives me her blessing and passes on the address. Another week passes. Up on a job at Cave Hill one day, I tell Diane I'm taking a break and pull into the drive. I'm nervous. I don't know how the wife is going to react to me. I don't want to make her cry. It's hot and the smell of lilac is overpowering. An orchid tree is in full bloom and some red hot pokers are thrusting into the air with the swagger of a youth giving the middle finger to life.

I knock on the door and the woman answers it. She looks calm, more groomed than the time I saw her before. The second she sees me, a smile spreads across her face and she says, 'I knew you'd come.'

She brings me into the living room. I can smell sweet pea. There are more orchids in pots and the whole effect is of life and growth.

I tell her what he'd said about loving her and the kids, and I talk of his passion for his novel. I see emotion in the lines of her face, but I don't want her to know I see it, so I keep my eyes tight on hers.

'It must have been a terrible shock to lose him like that,' I tell her.

'A shock?' she says. 'Not as much as you think. A few days before you saw him, we'd been told he had lung cancer. He'd been given only a couple of months to live. He could have died at any time.'

I couldn't believe it. 'So that's why he was in such a rush to finish the novel.'

'Yes, but I pleaded with him to stay. Either that or let me and the kids come with him.'

I remember her clearly now, the tears in her eyes at the front door. It's only now that I realise how much his dream had meant to him, how much it had cost him. To have it snatched away like that, along with his last chance to be with his family.

I hand her the novel and she holds it in her hands, before letting it slip onto the coffee table.

'Unfinished,' she says. 'So he failed in a way.'

'No,' I reply. 'To triumph is to try no matter what, right to the end. The book was never meant to be...'

It's the following week, the sun is splitting the trees and I'm back on the road.

A couple of American tourists fresh from a cruise ship bounce into the back and say, 'Take us to the Titanic.' They seem surprised when I tell them it sank a hundred years ago. I tell them all about our glorious past: 'Belfast used to be famous for its linen, rope and ships but all we're internationally recognised for now is trauma!'

It's about going the extra mile, giving the tourists the history to give myself the chance of a big tip. As my mother always says, 'You'd wear a good mouth out.' And yesterday I finally did it. I booked my round-the-world trip, put the down payment on it, and I'm really going.

Stop off at the Big Fish so the Americans can do a selfie. My God, faces as big as theirs should never be selfied, but, ah sure, makes them happy. They keep taking photos of me as I drive — I feel like I'm part of an art installation! Then on to the Balls on the Falls and the walls with all the murals and I'm just dreaming that in a few months' time I'll be seeing real murals like Michelangelo's in Rome. It's dreams like this that keep me working all day, I can't waste a minute now, I have to achieve it, and on this hot June night when I come home through my streets, I see that the local kids have been busy too and have set all the skips on fire. They're blazing away, flames cracking off the parched wood, the smoke rising into the clear sky like midsummer night dreams.

KETAMINE NIGHTS

I wake up and — where am I? where am I going in life? and it feels like I am on the verge of answering one of life's mysteries. Then I think harder and where I am is sprawled on a rumpled sofa and where I should be going this very day is to an interview for a teaching post at a school and I'm not communing with a higher force but with an old cushion, damp from my dribbles, with a dubious past.

It dawns on me exactly where I am — at Garrett and Emmy's cottage in Dundrum. Up on the ceiling is a layer of smog caused by record levels of tobacco, marijuana and salvia. It's ironic that most of the people here at the party are green in their politics but there you go. It's a hard one to throw an environmentally-friendly party. In the pursuit of hedonism, the polar ice caps have to go.

I try to remember how I got here. Ah, yes, I was walking down the Lisburn Road yesterday afternoon, thinking about my interview, when a car pulled up and Garrett called out, 'Fancy a wee kidnap?' Well, who wouldn't want to be smuggled away by a legendary party animal? Believe me, I would have kidnapped him myself to get to one of his parties and I thought to myself, sure I'm brilliantly prepared for this interview and if I go easy on it, all I'll end up with is a minor, manageable hangover.

I lift my head up, pain bubbling up in its core, and instantly I know why it's called a hangover as I want my life to be over and I want to hang myself. Oh God!

'The state of you,' someone laughs. I focus and it's Garrett, sitting perched on the arm of a chair, staring at me with wild, hyper-dilated eyes. His freckles are like sunbursts on his pale face. He thrusts a bottle into my hands. 'Here, Leah, get locked onto this.'

It's whiskey and I take a swift swig as I could do with a smoother-outer. My left foot is flapping like a fish and I slap it on the floor to stun it. What in hell's name did I take last night? I started on the beer, then... I do a quick inventory but paradoxically it's hard to remember memory-erasing substances. On the table lie all sorts of instruments of self-abuse: pipes, bongs, straws, rolled-up tenners... The carpet is littered with powder and herbal fragments and, no, these are not the spoors of your average party-goer but the tracks of the mega hell-rakers and psychedelic psychos holed up in Garrett and Emmy's cottage.

A two-year old, Willow, who belongs to a girl called Jenny, totters over and holds me out a bong. It's as if she knows.

I pick myself up from the grey, wrinkled sofa. It's like I've been sleeping with an extremely dishevelled pachyderm.

'Crazy night,' Garrett muses. 'Must have been the army with their sleeping mist.'

'Are you sure it wasn't the drugs?'

'Not a chance. The mist rolled in, then we all fell asleep.'

The cottage is right on the edge of the Ballykinler army base, but I'm less than convinced by his theory about the army doing experiments in chemical warfare on us. Personally, I think it's down to the chemicals flying round the party last night but I don't want to question it, given the insane stare of his eyes, so I go to the window as if searching for tell-tale signs of mist.

'Is that...helicopters?'

'Dirty bastards!' he yells, leaping up, shaking his fist. 'Fuck away off!"

He heads out the front door straight down the path to shout across the bay. He walks with this exaggerated stride like he's measuring out a field.

Wish I hadn't said a word. Logic is telling me they're probably birds with helicopter-like wings. Christ, last night's acid tab is still tweaking my brain. I head over to the sink for a pint of water, splashing some over my face. All I'm thinking of is making it to my interview. I check my watch. The hands are hurtling all over the place like needles on a Geiger counter, but finally they settle. 9.14 a.m. I have to be at Lagan College at 3, so at least I've plenty of time.

Jenny, a hippy hipster with a blond streak in her dark hair, holds out a tiny pill.

'No, put it away,' I say, my hands up in the air like she's holding a gun.

'It's fine,' she insists. 'It's a nox vomicum. Great for hangovers.'

'Oh, right. Well, it can't hurt,' I say, popping it.

She smiles fondly, as only an earth mother can. It's the first term of her homeopathy course. Perhaps I should be worried about being experimented upon but anything to try and shift this head of mine.

When I go back into the living room Emmy is sitting with Garrett, calming him down, stroking his hair. They're a strange couple these two, the doctor and the drug-dealer. A match made in heaven and hell really. He's so black haired; she's so golden blond. He's khaki shirts; she's lacy blouses. She temps as a doctor but she's on permanent call with Garrett. She's a one-woman ambulance. He used to be a heroin addict but he kicked it in and moved on to ketamine which Emmy nicks out of the hospital pharmacy. They are madly in love though and their looks of adoration almost make me envious.

Conan comes in, announcing he's starving. I'm way past hunger pains, having been on the A-Z Drug Diet for the past eighteen hours, but on the good side at least I'll be slim for my interview.

Emmy and I follow Conan into the kitchen. In real life he's a chef at a posh bistro. He spots some dried magic mushrooms on the sideboard that would make a good core ingredient. Everything in the fridge is past its sell-by date but Emmy says it's all good, it's just the multi-million-dollar food industry conning us into buying new stuff. According to her, even the lumps in the milk are wonderful for our immune systems.

'Right. I can't cook on an empty stomach,' says Conan, pouring himself a glass of cider and bolting it down before he starts. Fortified, he speed-chops potatoes and an onion.

'Do you want a cider too, Leah?' Emmy asks.

'Why not ? Might help with the hangover.'

'Sure hangovers are great,' Emmy says. 'They're just nature's way of revealing to us the pain of existence. How else can you find empathy for others?'

She's empathetic enough herself to hand me a vitamin C with my cider, but just then Jenny comes up and swipes it.

'Sorry,' she says, 'but my need is greater than yours.'

She explains she's just remembered she slept with one of the guys here last night and needs as much vitamin C as she can get — she read all about how great it was in a book called *The Herbal Abortionist.*

'I hope to God this works,' she says, necking about half the jar, then trotting off to the bathroom to insert the rest vaginally.

'Never mind, Leah. I've something else for you,' says Emmy with an angelic smile.

She takes me outside. The mist on the sea is being burnt off by the April sun. Dundrum Bay is glorious, the gorse and buckthorn flowers almost phosphorescent in their glow. She takes me into a tiny outhouse, shows me some dark brown bottles and says it's Garrett's homebrew. He's actually fermenting rainwater with yeast and sugar. Yep, trust Garrett to come up with a plan to turn water into wine. When Emmy opens it, *POP*, the blast's so powerful the cork almost takes out a seagull.

She passes me the bottle. The first swallow and the top of my head blasts off. No, I mustn't freak out. I must NOT freak out. I casually run my hand over my skull and realise the damage is only on the inside. That I can cope with. I start to have images of diving into a taxi to Dundrum, then catching a bus to Belfast. Time's marching on and I'm hoping a few of the partygoers crashed out in the bedroom will resurface soon and drive me back. I know, I just know, I can make that interview as long as I don't drink any more. Admittedly my breath's like a brewery but that's easily sorted by chewing on a couple of cloves.

When we go back in, Jenny's kissing Conan amidst the hisses and bubbles of the pots and pans. Her glasses are steamed up, whether from the cooking or the kissing I can't tell. After downing all that vitamin C, she's on to her next man.

Garrett and Emmy's dog, Socks, who is so-called because of his white paws, starts licking my hand in sympathy. Suddenly I love that dog. I *love* that dog.

'Brunch is served!' calls Conan, though really it is more of a drunch — drugs and lunch.

'It's actually dreakfast,' says Emmy.

We all sit down at the table, our dysfunctional druggie family, to magic mushroom soup. Willow is chewing on a rusk. Jenny's freaking out because she can't find the packet she had containing her last three bumbles, but Emmy says even in the unlikely event that Willow has necked them she'll probably be alright.

'Sure she ate five paracetamol at our last party,' points out Emmy, 'and she was grand.'

I can't help thinking social services should be involved but, after all, Emmy is a doctor and I'm in no fit state to be a moral paragon.

'This soup's class, isn't it?' says Garrett. 'I bulked it up with a few temazies when Conan wasn't looking.'

'You fucking bastard!' cries Conan, who's already wolfed his bowl down. 'If you came into my restaurant kitchen and did that I'd kill you.'

'It still tastes wonderful.' Emmy flashes a conciliatory smile.

'Maybe I should have put in speed,' Garrett wonders. 'Easier for doing the dishes.'

'I don't think I'll make my interview now,' I comment, looking regretfully at my half-finished bowl. I'm beginning to feel I've just floated off the world into gravity.

'Great,' grins Garrett. 'You can stay and take part in the Temazie 500 instead.'

I go to the back door and phone the principal's secretary at Lagan College. It takes me three goes to press in the numbers. I say to myself, focus, Leah, focus.

'I'm really, really sorry about this short notice,' I say, 'but this terrible flu has come over me and I'm not going to be able to make this afternoon's interview.'

'Yes, you do sound a bit groggy,' she says.

'I've just taken a couple of pills,' I tell her, and the truth of it pleases me.

'No probs,' she says brightly. 'We can fit you in Monday if you think you'll be well enough by then.'

'Brilliant,' I agree with alacrity. It's Friday afternoon, so surely I will have escaped here by Monday, as long as they stop spiking my food. I mean, hospitable is good but Garrett takes hosting to a whole new level. He's worse than Mrs Doyle from *Father Ted*.

Back in the kitchen, Emmy with a shriek grabs a sharp knife away from Willow's hands. She looks around for acknowledgement but saving lives can go seriously underappreciated round here.

'Well done, you,' I tell her.

After dreakfast, Garrett rounds up a couple of crashed-out guys and a girl from the spare bedroom, tossing them a few temazies. Then he ushers us out into the field at the back of his house. Amazing— he's built us a mini-assault course. Inspired by his fears of the British

Army, we are the start of his own private army, us band of red-eyed, deadbeat, high-as-a-kite, tatterdemalion wastrels.

'You're in fine condition for the Temazie 500,' he tells us motivatingly. 'Sure they fed them LSD in Vietnam! Right, troops, here is the starting line. On your marks. Get set, go!'

We start to run but the ground is quicksand. The temazies are kicking in good-style. Emmy grabs onto my leg, hoping to be dragged along. Garrett has fallen over the logs up ahead and is crawling over them with the speed of a sloth. Jeff Buckley's 'Hallelujah' is blaring out from the kitchen. The event has all the surreal beauty of a delicious nightmare.

It's a straight race up ahead between Jenny and Garrett but Jenny streaks ahead. Garrett, the cheating bastard, takes his boot off and chucks it at the finishing line. We watch in horror at the slowmo trajectory of the boot which arcs against the blue sky and heads unerringly towards Jenny. The boot lands with a thunk on the side of Jenny's head and fells her. Willow who is cheering on her Mummy, emits a large wail while Jenny, prone on the soil, tries to console her. Meanwhile Emmy staggers over to rescue Garrett from drowning in a puddle.

Garrett declares himself the victor and suggests we all have a swimming race next. Emmy scotches it as a bad idea, citing Jeff Buckley who died at thirty after going swimming on drink and drugs. Thank God for Emmy. Her full name is Emmeline which reminds me of a Victorian heroine.

A rat-a-tat-tat pierces the air from the army shooting range nearby and I kind of understand why Garrett's so hyped and nervous. It's like living in a warzone.

'So, what shall we do instead?' asks Jenny brightly.

'Hang the host?' suggests Conan.

'Yeah, let's hang Emmy!' cries Garrett and Emmy starts to run.

Conan grabs Emmy's blouse which rips as she tries to wriggle away. Garrett disappears into the outhouse to emerge with a rope.

Fuck sake, this can't be happening!

In the middle of the melee, I can see a guy sneak over to his car. My brain may be mushed from the mushrooms but I can see he's doing a runner and I go as fast as I can after him and wrench open the passenger door.

'Let's fly!' I say, jumping in.

The car refuses to start first go. I look out the rear window. Garrett is throwing the rope round a branch while Conan and Jenny drag Emmy towards it. All of them are laughing, smiling with devilment.

The car starts this time but the wheel spins in the mud. Garrett spots us and comes running up as we keep revving. Suddenly we're off but Garrett leaps like a flying salmon onto the windscreen.

'You're not fucking going!' Garrett is shouting.

'Jesus fuck!' says the guy next to me, but he keeps his foot to the floor as the wheels screech onto the country lane and Garrett is about to slide off the bonnet but he grabs on to the windscreen wipers. One of them snaps off and Garrett goes flying into the ditch.

'Cunts!' he shouts, leaping up.

We head on, us fleeing fugitives, and I look back at the cottage and I can see them all, Emmy hanging by her waist from the tree, Jenny and Willow waving at us and it's like I'm running away from myself, and it's like this monstrous, cloven-hoofed side of me is still there, and I'm half-sad and half-jubilant to be leaving.

The guy next to me is cute and has the beard of an urban hipster.

'Cracking wee party,' he says.

I look straight ahead, the remains of the windscreen wiper sticking up like an antenna. And all around me the countryside is pulsating with blossom and there's nothing like a bout of self-destructiveness to make you feel truly alive, and, if there's one thing I know, I don't want to be sitting in a classroom on a Friday afternoon ever again.

'Cracking alright,' I say.

THE LOST GENERATION

As she walked into the La Mon, a hedonistic dance anthem was pumping out of one of the private rooms. It clearly didn't belong to her reunion though she would have laughed if it had. She didn't know why they'd chosen the La Mon anyway, as it never had the best of vibes about it since the bombing. All day she'd been keyed up, wondering who'd be there. Twenty-five years was a ferociously long time. And even if you didn't show it much on the surface, the years were there somewhere inside you, like growth rings in a tree.

She saw the sign for her school and went in. A woman in heavy make-up let out a cry of delight and grabbed her.

'Kate!'

Deep in the clinch, Kate didn't have a clue who it was. The woman pointed to her name badge.

'I'm Nina. Don't you remember me?'

She could see the disappointment in Nina's eyes. She played an image of the more reticent, eighteen-year-old Nina alongside this blond, sexualized woman. It didn't really compute except for the same fun in the eyes.

'Yeah, Nina, of course! It's just your hair's all straightened now,' added Kate to soften the let-down. 'So, what are you up to?'

'I'm a yoga teacher.'

'Married?'

'Divorced, one daughter. But I got the house,' she crowed, 'so it's all good.'

Kate bought a pint and was buffeted by the force of Nina's enthusiasm through several groups of old classmates. Her closest friends from school weren't there. The women who'd turned up had tinted, straightened hair and plucked eyebrows, and the ghosts of their teenage faces only played in their smiles.

Kate gravitated immediately towards Lisa, the wild girl who'd been expelled. Lisa was wearing bohemian black, but anticlimactically revealed that she was a teacher now. Surely one of us, Kate thought to herself, could have been a brothel keeper or a computer hacker — a terrorist at the very least!

Some of the men were unrecognizable without their puppy fat. Alan 'M-acne-roy' McIlroy, as he'd been cruelly renamed back then, looked good now and you could hardly make out the scars under his hipsteresque stubble. In a misguided effort to be comic, he was wearing his old school tie. He screwed his eyes up when he was introduced to Kate, trying to place her. All it took was one puzzled glance to turn the night into a bruising arena, dispelling the illusion of how popular you were at school and reminding you of your own insignificance.

'There's Mark Matthews,' Nina pointed out excitedly. 'Let's go over.'

Mark Matthews had possessed chiselled, heroin-chic good looks. The man of the same name was tubby and balding but turned the same intense eyes on them.

'God, you used to be the school stud!' exclaimed Kate with too much surprise for Mark's liking.

'Yeah,' he said almost sheepishly.

'You had sex with Miss Kernaghan, didn't you?'

'I was having *a lot* of sex back then,' he grinned.

Kate kept playing a fragmented film of the past in her mind alongside the present; it was like the room was in split screen. She found a moment to escape on her own. Along the corridor, the dance music was still thumping. A couple of teenagers bounded out of the room, buzzing. They looked at her and giggled, their cheeks round and full, their lips like overripe fruit, like they could burst at any second.

It was late September. She drove Dan up the winding lane to Dundrum Castle, a faint sweetness in the air from the tangled bank of blackberries. It had been an achingly long summer between the end of school and the start of university but it was now her last night and she was packed to go to Bristol the next morning. Dan was leaving for London in a few days himself.

They reached the locked gates of the castle and she turned the car so it looked out over Dundrum Bay. They seemed to be the only ones there, though you never knew if a few glue-sniffers were hanging round the keep. In the distance, they could see the lights from the army base in Ballykinler reflected in iridescent shards on the dark water. The soldiers were shooting flares into the sky.

'Northern Ireland's version of a son et lumière,' joked Kate wryly. 'I'll miss it.'

'I got a leaving gift for you,' Dan said, digging a box out of his shirt pocket.

She opened it to find a brooch he'd made for her. It was a tiny feather with strokes of colour through it; one of the feathers he used for fly fishing.

'It's beautiful.'

He kissed her. She could feel his pent-up frustration. He'd kissed her for the first time some weeks ago and it had been rough too. It was just him; the way he'd walked through the school corridors with a long, urgent stride like he wanted to move quickly in life and couldn't wait. She pressed back hard too, grabbing the back of his neck. He pushed a hand in under her top; the other slipped down the front of her jeans.

'Can we all sit down for dinner, please?' said Ruth, who'd organized the reunion and seemed to be glorying a bit too much in reliving her role as head girl.

There was a cutesy touch of lots of retro sweets on the tables— Black Jacks, Fruit Salads, Refreshers, Love Hearts, Parma Violets...

Just then, Dan came in. She felt a heat rise in her chest as he walked over and hugged her.

'Kate, it's so great to see you.'

Ruth's voice barked out, 'Dan and Kate, could you sit down please?'

Dan tried to join another table of lads but there were no free seats, so, embarrassed, he sat down beside Kate after all. Kate looked at his wedding ring. She'd heard he'd married years ago from one of her relatives in Dundrum, so it wasn't a surprise. He hadn't changed much apart from a few flecks of grey and a few light lines round his eyes; upturned ones like ticks, no crosses.

'So, what are you up to?' he asked.

The truth was she was employed for only ten hours a week lecturing in English. She was part of the academic precariat and had just spent the summer on the dole, but there was no way she was going to admit it.

'Lecturing at Queen's,' she replied, trying to move on quickly. 'And you? Last time I heard you were working on oil rigs.'

'Yeah, but I got made redundant. It was great—I was in Africa and Iraq.'

He told her eagerly all about Kenya. During a scary dispute he'd taken spears and knives off the workers.

She noticed that his blue eyes were bloodshot. It was probably nothing but it looked like he hadn't slept all night, or he'd been crying or drinking.

'So what do you do now?' she asked.

'I make seats for airplanes in Kilkeel. They employ eight hundred people there. It's huge.'

'Next time I'm on a plane,' she flirted, 'I'll imagine your hands were on my very seat.'

'You do that,' he laughed.

Nina started reminiscing at the table about how Kate had got her into trouble for mimicking a teacher.

'Hmm. Not like you to get into trouble, was it, Kate?' Dan teased.

It was strange but she couldn't remember being part of Nina's story. She looked at Dan and wondered if her memories of him were real.

After dinner, she followed him to the bar.

'You haven't changed a bit, you know,' he smiled.

'Well, you have.'

She lightly touched the ring on his finger. He hid his face in his Guinness, not wanting to talk about it.

'How many kids?' she asked.

'Four. I put the oldest on the road this year. Cost a lot, driving lessons.'

An image flashed into Kate's mind of being in the car with him. Of the feel of his body.

'No kids for me. I always wanted to be free.'

'I know,' he nodded. 'I'm just so glad, Kate, you're doing well.'

'You too.'

'What, me?' His voice darkened. 'God, I hate my job. I work at a factory, I'm sitting in with my family every night. Before, I would travel, I was free for months at a time. Do you know what I do now? I go to Ballykinler and I take my knife and I hack and hack through the shrubs, just hack and hack for hours.'

'Hey, Dan!'

Alan bounced over to him and she drifted away. Nearby, Nina was showing off like mad, hoiking up her skirt and doing the splits in front of everyone. Some of the women looked horrified but the men were mesmerized — it was fun to have a bit of train-wreck madness.

'Hey, Nina,' she called out. 'Love the Las Vegas floor show.'

'Christ, did you just see me?' Nina giggled. 'It was their fault for asking about my yoga moves.'

Her teeth were dark from the Black Jacks and the red wine. Kate could see the prickling roughness of the skin under Nina's make-up and guessed that alcohol use had turned her into the exhibitionist she was now.

'You looked brilliant,' she said, wanting to be kind. 'I couldn't have done the splits even when I was at school.'

'Neither could I!' replied Nina.

While the men stood chatting at the bar, the women remained seated, tethered by their high heels. It reminded Kate of the old division of the sexes in the sixth form common room. It was getting late but no one would leave. It was like they were waiting for something.

Alan McIlroy was talking about one of their year who'd died in his twenties. Ciaran had been knocked down on a road in Spain and killed. They all shivered. Alan's wife was beside him, nodding. She was from Brazil and she was tactile. Kate felt her long, sweeping stroke on her bare arm.

'I wonder if we'll all be here at our thirtieth reunion,' said Alan.

'Well, I'll not be here,' Kate told him, thinking one reunion was enough.

'Oh, you will,' Dan said and she wondered why he was so insistent. 'We'll all be here.'

A couple of the non-drinking Presbyterians were leaving early. They signalled to Dan.

'Kate, I've got to go now,' he explained regretfully. 'They're giving me a lift back to Newcastle.'

'Oh. You have to?'

'Yes.'

He kissed her on the cheek.

He was kissing and pressing her hard. His fingers ground against her so much it hurt, but it was a fiery hurt that thrilled her. His eyes were half-closed like he was in a trance. He tried to move her jeans down her thighs, but she made her body a deadweight, suddenly scared of him. What if he made her pregnant? All she could think was she was leaving for Bristol and wasn't coming back. As all the teachers had said, 'Go. Everywhere's better than here. You can't even get a job here because of the Troubles.'

The gunfire rat-a-tatted across the bay from Ballykinler. She really liked Dan but she didn't want him to be waiting, tying her with his expectation.

At her retreat, Dan's touches faded, his kissing ebbed. His fingers stroked her face.

'I'll see you at Christmas, but if you like I could come up from London and visit you.'

'I don't know,' she answered. She started the car. 'I'd better get back. I'm up at five.'

The stars were pinholing brightly through the black sky as though telling her that God's light was behind everything. Just like she'd outgrown school, she'd outgrown Dundrum. She couldn't even contemplate what she wanted out of life because even to start thinking of things, it felt like her heart was exploding with its own power.

The car wheeled down Castle Hill to the Main Street.

He was quiet. She could feel the tension in him.

Birds hooted across the bay.

'You could come back to my house if you want,' he said.

'No. I've got to go home.'

It was ironic, thought Kate. You turn someone down only to be turned down by him twenty-five years later.

She was barely listening to Nina's recollections. They were about how she used to dance on the dining room table with her dinner guests; a party trick her ex hadn't found remotely amusing. Nina kept looking at Mark Matthews. She licked her red wine lips like a vampire feasting and muttered that she was going out with him for a smoke.

Kate felt an arm grab hers and she swung round. It was Dan, his eyes shining.

'I didn't say goodbye to you.'

'You did.' He looked drunk but then everyone was pretty drunk by now.

'Not properly.'

He hugged her and kissed her hard on the lips. She could feel her skin crushed against her teeth; that tiny bit of pain that proved you were alive.

And then he was gone.

The classmates all drank together for a couple more hours, still waiting, still yearning for something. The barman let them stock up on double pints when he called last orders. They talked about the ones who went to England and the USA for work and never came back; half a generation had been lost.

'The funny thing was the teachers lied,' Kate mused, 'when they said England would be better than here.'

'To think at eighteen we were going to set fire to the world,' romanticised Lisa.

'Christ sake,' Kate laughed. 'We'd need a fire lit under our chairs now!'

She finally stumbled into her taxi at about three.

'Where are you from?' the taxi driver asked, detecting the

English traces in her voice from having lived there for years.

'Here. From County Down, originally.'

'You don't sound County Down. What part?'

'All of me,' she quipped and the taxi driver smiled. But she could see him looking at her in the mirror, still wondering, still hoping to establish a kinship.

The late September weather had changed. A leaf slapped against the windscreen like a clammy hand. The limbs were flailing on the trees that lined the country roads back into Belfast. A couple of branches were sheered clean off and the taxi driver swerved to avoid them. The leaves fizzled and fomented on boughs that hacked and hacked and hacked at the wind.

'Wild, isn't it?' she said, looking out.

'Wild,' said the taxi driver.

ACKNOWLEDGEMENTS

Acknowledgements are due to the following in which versions of these stories were first published or broadcast: 'Bomb Dust' was published in *Belfast Stories* (Doire Press, 2019); and 'Two People Shorten the Road' was broadcast on BBC Radio 4 in August, 2018.

Enduring thanks to Damian Smyth and the Arts Council of Northern Ireland for funding the writing of these short stories through the support of a General Arts Award in 2016. Thanks also to Lisa Frank and John Walsh for continuing to be my publishers and to all the mad folk of Belfast who eternally entertain and inspire.

ROSEMARY JENKINSON was born in Belfast and is an award-winning playwright and short story writer. Her plays include *The Bonefire* (Stewart Parker BBC Radio Award), *Planet Belfast, Here Comes the Night, Michelle and Arlene, Dream, Sleep, Connect* and *Lives in Translation*. She was 2017 Artist-in-Residence at the Lyric Theatre in Belfast. Rosemary's short story collections include *Contemporary Problems Nos. 53 & 54* (Lagan Press, 2004), *Aphrodite's Kiss* (Whittrick Press, 2016) and *Catholic Boy* (Doire Press, 2018), which was shortlisted for the EU Prize for Literature. She was singled out by *The Irish Times* for 'an elegant wit, terrific characterisation and an absolute sense of her own particular Belfast'. In 2018 she received a Major Individual Artist Award from the Arts Council of Northern Ireland to write a memoir.